Lost Orbit

PETER J. OSTERLUND

For those feeling lost in the universe, you are not alone.

Contents

Prologue

Across the endless sky of stars and planets, a ship suddenly appeared within the Milky Way galaxy, heading towards Earth with incredible velocity.

Normally, the ship's pilots would begin entering the final stages of space-way several parsecs back, but with their tight schedule, they allowed the ship to fly.

At least for another minute.

The pilots were conducting their weekly shipment for Earth, delivering the same necessities as all the other hundreds of star systems needed nowadays: plastic, raw materials, oxygen—everything considered essential.

In hindsight, the pilots were only a couple of minutes off schedule. Unfortunately, even that was enough to make a difference.

"You just had to ask for her contact, didn't you?" The captain said, turning back to his copilot, who, judging from his undone fly, had just returned from the washroom.

"Oh, but you had to see her man," the copilot said, "she was—."

"I don't care what she was. You and her are the reason we're late. Damn, corporate is going to be on my ass if we don't get there on time."

A brief pause went on as the copilot sat in his seat, "We coming up to planet three yet?"

"Yes," The captain nodded, "we should be seeing Earth in three, two, one...".

The intoxicating sensation of space-way stopped as the pilot pulled back the hydraulics throttle, causing him and his coworker to test the steadiness and capabilities of their chairs. The flashes of light in front of them were replaced with darkness, filled with twinkles of starlight and distant planets.

To an untrained eye, the sight would appear completely normal; however, both pilots could tell something was off.

"Mac," the captain called to his copilot, "Where are we?"

Mac looked puzzled, "What do you mean?"

"I mean, what is our current location?"

"We're within the Milky Way galaxy, between the planets Venus and Mars." Mac could tell something was wrong but failed to understand what it was. "What's the matter, Rook?"

Rook turned away from the glass screen separating the vacuum of space from him and Mac. His face was a deep red that pulsed along his forehead and eyes. At first, Mac assumed that Rook hadn't taken too kindly from coming out of Space-way, after all, it was easy to forget just how hard space travel could affect the human body.

But unfortunately, Mac realised soon enough that that was not the case. His captain was furious. And as was usually the case, Mac was the cause of it.

"Where is Earth?" Rook exploded as he pointed towards the open space.

"I...I don't know." Mac stuttered, "Maybe we passed it. Or maybe—."

"Or maybe *someone* put in the wrong coordinates."

This was not at all what he needed right now. Not only was Rook going to be late, but he was lost and in need of resupplying if they needed to jump into space-way again.

The two stood there awkwardly without a sound. Space always had a way of causing such silences.

Rook took a single step closer to Mac before speaking in a far more controlled manner, "Find out where we are."

"Yes, sir." Mac nodded before leaving the cockpit.

Rook watched as the cause of his problems left him alone, contemplating whether or not he should let Mac go. *Two years on the job and he still fails to do even the simplest...* Rook's thoughts were interrupted as he stared up, catching a glimpse of the reflection on a screen. There was an orb, floating perfectly still at the centre of the screen. It was an aged grey, and the surface of the orb looked fractured, like a rock that had just been nicked at with a mining tool. Rook knew what it was before he turned around to see a clearer view of it. Everyone would be able to recognise such a thing.

The moon, Earth's moon, was floating there before him, clear as day, with the sun's light bouncing off its surface.

It can't be; Rook moved quickly to the surface of the cockpit. His face leaned up against it, causing his breath to fog up the glass. He looked to his left, then right, searching for any evidence of their current location.

The pilot dropped back into his chair before signalling the ship that they were about to move. Rook was tempted not to give Mac the warning but inevitably thought of a far worse punishment for him.

He took the steering wheel, pulling it towards him as he pushed the hydraulics throttle forward, just enough to send him forward to the moon in a matter of seconds.

Even with over twenty years of piloting under him, Rook still never got over the speed of ships and space travel. To him, it felt like bending the rules of reality itself. Nothing was supposed to move with such speed, nothing. Yet here he was, driving a ship four kilometres long towards the moon.

The moon was just what Rook thought it to be, Earth's moon, the one first walked on by man over five thousand years ago.

He could still see the planted flag, as well as the ancient technology left there. Even after all this time, there was no use in coming back to the moon; there was no possible usefulness or reason for visiting the grey orb. It was best to leave it be and to let it function with the planet it was allocated to for all this time. But the question was, where was its planet? Where was Earth?

Rook turned away from the moon, surveying whatever was around it in terms of planets or artificial landscapes. If this was truly the Milky Way galaxy, then surely there would be...Rook gasped as he saw the sun and the first two planets in front of it.

Mercury and Venus.

They were both separated by great distances in their orbit, with Venus blocking a measly part of the great star, while Mercury was just barely visible from behind. *What...what the?* Rook's hands were now shaking. He blinked before letting go of the ship's control, slowing it down to a complete stop. He pressed one of the buttons above him, causing a voice to sound.

"Hello sir, how can I assist you?"

"Dallas," Rook said, "Run a space scan for me, will you? Find out where the hell we are."

"At once, sir."

The ship's A.I was not at all slow to complete its search, unlike Mac. However, in the end, they both returned to Rook with the same result.

"Sir," Mac said, out of breath with a face of pure white. "We...we're at the right galactic coordinates."

"What?" Rook asked with disbelief. He already knew the fearful answer but hoped for some other logical explanation. Dallas, the ship's A.I was of no help with its extensive report either.

"*Sir,*" Dallas called, "*We are currently within the Milky Way galaxy, floating in the space between Earth and its moon.*"

"This doesn't make any sense," Rook said to himself, "Dallas, where is Earth, the planet 0003?"

The A.I was silent for some time; it was too much time for any artificial intelligence.

Eventually, it spoke with a hesitant voice. "*I...I'm not sure.*"

Mac gasped this time, looking to his boss for the answers but seeing no sign of receiving any.

"Mac," Rook had a stern look now, disguising his incomprehensible anxiety. "Send a distress call to all sectors of the Cosmos Order."

"What should I tell them?"

"Tell them that..." He knew no matter how it was worded, it would sound ridiculous. He bit his lip before continuing, "Tell them...the Earth has disappeared."

Chapter One

Universal News

The entire universe had learned about Earth's disappearance.

So far, there had been no distress calls found from the residents of Earth, nor any forms of communication.

As far as everyone in the universe knew, the origin of humanity had disappeared.

Numerous theories surfaced throughout Cosmos Order's star systems, attempting to conclude what could have caused Earth's disappearance. And more importantly, where was its current location? Most of them were of no validity, explaining that Earth was swallowed by its sun or that Earth had never truly existed and was a planet made up by the Order. That theory had gained some traction as the majority of the universe's inhabitants had never seen, let alone stood on the first planet of humanity.

Despite all the chaos and confusion that spread throughout the universe, life was still able to go on. For some.

Meanwhile, on a distant planet called Haple, a lecture was taking place at the University of Rentwich, located in the planet's southern regions. Haple was a rather small planet, almost half the size of Earth; however, that isn't to say it was limited in scale. The world itself was a global metropolis, holding no buildings that stood shorter than five stories.

It was an overwhelming place to live in, but then again, that was the reason why Doctor Reed Doyle had moved there. He needed somewhere crowded, somewhere populated by tens of billions. He needed to hide from the Cosmos Order.

Especially now with Earth missing.

Dr Doyle's lecture on matter distribution had concluded, leaving him with very little work to assign his five remaining students. He always found himself shaking his head, especially now with the current disaster going on with Earth, that there had been a lack of interest in astro-physics and science as a whole.

Everyone nowadays pursued politics or galactic bounty hunting, two careers that held no level of respect, at least from the likes of Doctor Doyle.

With the rest of the day, Reed had very little to do with his time besides lying low.

I ought to shave, he thought as he caught a glimpse of himself in one of the window's reflections.

Reed hated how dirty a beard or even a stubble looked on him. Along with his perfectly round glasses and thinning hair, it was not a look he desired.

But then again, if it came down to being recognised by the Order or having to scratch his chin fifty times a day, he would always pick the latter.

With the afternoon just arriving on Haple's thirty-two-hour day, he decided to travel to the park, one of the few found on the city-based planet. From there, he would sit and read the paper.

Despite his rather young age of thirty standard years, Reed couldn't help but feel old, the way the locals always looked up to him from their Artificial Information Multitool, or A.I.M as it was casually referred to.

To them, paper was a foreign thing, a thing of the past. But Reed appreciated having the paper in his hands, of feeling the smooth, fresh skin of a tree tickle his fingertips. Technology, to him, was something that had advanced both beautifully and horrifically, becoming something humanity could no longer live without.

The words printed in the newspaper were nothing short of dreadful, speaking yet again of the crisis of Earth's disappearance. *They still haven't found it;* the doctor's heart skipped a beat as he read the article heading, 'Still no sign of Earth.'

·There were obvious reasons why he felt the way he did with Earth's current situation. For one, it was his home world, the place in which he lived for the first fifteen standard years of his life.

The other reason for Reed's worrying was that he knew *they* would soon be after him. With a dilemma such as this, they would need the most brilliant astrophysicist and planetologist of this time.

No. That's not what I do, not anymore.

Whether it was because of a change in the artificial wind of the city or the divine intuition Reed always believed he possessed, he felt that something was off.

He stretched the paper wide enough so that it hid his profile. There was no reason for him to feel paranoid, not yet at least, but still, he couldn't shake the feeling.

Slowly, he lowered the paper.

No one was around, no one except the few who were glued to the screen of their A.I.M devices, watching and communicating to others across the universe instantaneously.

Reed brushed his hair back, sighing away the worry.

Any day the Order could find him and bring him in for all he'd done.

Why shouldn't they? A part of him thought. *I deserve some punishment for what I've done, don't I?* Reed folded the newspaper up and left his rather comfortable spot.

When he first arrived on Haple, Doctor Doyle had made it a goal of his to lose the habit of looking over his shoulder. He knew the action only succeeded in making him appear all the more suspicious to any agents of the Order. But given some time and an eyebrow-raising amount of practice, Reed was able to walk like a soldier.

Unfortunately for today, old habits were returning, and worries he had long forgotten about were coming back to haunt him.

Not again, the doctor thought, *never again will I help a world.*

Reed groaned as he looked over his shoulder once more, hoping it would relieve him of the panic he was feeling. It didn't; if anything, it just made him sweat all the more profusely. The real stab of fear was when he turned the corner towards his apartment, eyeing a pair of black-suited men who wore a reform disc on their forefingers.

Reed stopped at the sight. *Do they plan to attack me?*

The two suits looked immediately in Reed's direction, eyeing him coldly as though they were informed of his expected whereabouts. Doyle turned away, ready to run in the opposite direction of the men, but before he could, a pair of hands gripped him by his shoulders.

"Doctor Doyle, I presume." A voice came from behind Reed, "Why don't we have a chat."

"We can chat here," Doyle replied with a dry mouth.

Another suit, Reed eyed the man. *How many of them are there?*

The suited man glanced around himself and Reed, noticing a crowd beginning to film the exchange. "It's of a rather confidential matter."

"And if I choose not to comply?" Doyle asked.

The man laughed, "Then you'll be arrested for treason, failure to arrive at court, bypassing a series of space borders, murder, theft, and a dozen additional crimes."

Oh yeah, Reed remembered all of his criminal acts, even the ones the suit hadn't mentioned.

"Do we have an understanding?" The suit asked, knowing full and well Doyle didn't have a choice. The Doctor nodded before being escorted to the suit's ship.

The suits took Reed to the closest detention centre, located across the planet in the city of Yort. Reed had never been there personally, but to him, it looked all the same, the way the city was clustered with sky-high buildings and fifty-metre-tall flatscreens that always blinded him with their neon lights.

The Doctor sat in a compact interrogation room. He couldn't help but laugh as the room looked so much like those found within his collection of films back at his apartment. *I wonder if they'll go for the good cop, bad cop approach. Or maybe they'll just start pummelling me until I comply.*

Reed took his glasses off, wiping away any marks he could see on either of the perfectly round lenses. He almost dropped them as the door slammed open, announcing his interrogator.

Only one suited man entered the room. With him, he held a thick binder.

"Doctor Reed Doyle," The suit said, "The rogue planetologist." He dropped the binder on the desk before pushing towards Reed. "Open it."

Reed paused, not from the binder but from the sight of the suit's black eyes. Reed had never felt comfortable with being in the same room as Androids, but he knew he had no choice but to do as he was told.

He opened the binder. The first page was a transcript recorded a week ago from a delivery ship that had departed from Haple and arrived in the Milky Way galaxy. However, it failed to meet its destination.

"Earth," Doyle said, looking up from the binder back to the piercing pits of the android's robotic eyes.

"Yes." The Android sat down opposite Reed, "I take it you've heard the concerning news involving it."

"Of course. Everyone has."

The android hummed between breaths.

Reed stirred in his seat. It was irritating to see something lifeless inhaling air. The function was utterly useless, with the small exception of making people all the more com-fortable. "Then you know why we need you," The android said.

"*We?*"

"The Order. We need your...skills to find the planet. Or at least learn about what has become it."

"I'm not a detective you know," Reed said.

"No, but you are a rather brilliant planetologist. Your resumé alone is enough to convince anyone you're up for the job."

"My resumé or my record?" Doyle asked.

"Both," The android smiled, "You've had quite the ca-reer with only a handful of years under your belt." Reed's eyes darted at the suit, not wanting to hear his so-called achievements. "There was the prevention of the colonial wars of asphalt, the blocking of carbon monoxide on Tui II, and the removal of the planetary tumour at Xesas. Oh, what else was there? I'm forgetting one, aren't I?" The Android began to rub its chin as if human thinking was something it was capable of. "The First rains of Strand?"

Reed nodded, embarrassed of how envious the android appeared. *They don't know about the other planet. I hope.*

The suit continued, "Of course, with every achievement, there is some form of setback. Isn't that right?"

"So you've said. I fail to understand the relevancy, though." Reed flicked through the pages of the binder still in front of him.

"Well, that's what I was getting at, Doctor." The android slapped the binder with the palm of its hand, causing Reed to jump. The suit pulled the binder back towards him and closed it. "The Cosmos Order is willing to offer you a deal, one I think you should consider very much."

"What deal?" Reed asked.

The android smiled all the more menacingly than before. "You have a choice; you can help the Order, either by finding Earth or learning what happened to it, if indeed it was destroyed, as many have theorised. Do this, and all your past crimes and current warrants against you will be diminished. You will be pardoned, effective immediately upon accomplishing your mission."

Ignored until called upon, the words of an old friend had echoed in Reed's head throughout his years in hiding, dreadfully anticipating a day such as today when he would be forced to help yet another planet. *I swore to never again help a world. Never.*

"And if I don't?" Reed asked, waiting for the answer he knew would turn his stomach.

"Your crimes alone accumulate to over ten centuries of imprisonment; most men begin to attempt suicide after only half of one on the dreaded planet." It was no secret that the prison planet, Eion, was a damned system, one that reshaped a person horrifically in mind, body, and soul as they were forced to ingest the life-extending medicinals inside their food and drinks. But the real horror of Eion was that none of the prisoners could die. Pain, fear, and other sufferings of the human body were still apparent, but death, the choice of cutting one's punishment short, of possessing the will to decide when enough was enough and to end it all, that was stripped from the prisoners. Everyone who'd either heard or had been sent to the prison planet knew death was the better path.

Reed knew much about Eion. Back when the Order and Reed were on good terms, he had helped bring in numerous felons, all of whom had been involved in planetary crimes.

Reed felt forced to pour himself a glass of water. For all he knew, it could very well be his last fulfilling drink.

Reed swallowed, "What about good behaviour?" he asked, testing the android's understanding of sarcasm.

The android threw its head back far enough that it lifted the front two legs of its chair. "Good behaviour," he echoed, "that's rich. Even if such a thing were possible for deathless imprisonment, you'd still be facing two to three centuries in a cell. Is that really what you want for yourself?"

That still wouldn't be enough for the pain I've caused, Reed thought, his hands turning white as he clenched them atop the table.

"I take it we agree then, Doctor." The suit began to leave the room.

"If I...," Reed began, stopping the android, "If I fail to help the Order, if I am unable to find or learn about what happened to Earth, what then?"

The android smiled once more, winking one of its space-black eyes at Reed, "Then to Eion you go, with an updated list of accomplishments to accompany you."

Chapter Two
Response

Doyle could still remember the last time he'd been granted an armed escort. Of course, it had been under far different circumstances and with a more vocal company.

The suit's listing of Reed's past accomplishments reminded him of the time he had been sent to talk with the clans of planet Asphalt, where he discussed possible ways to avert the rumoured war and save the planet from catastrophe. Back then, Reed was seen as a significant individual within the Order, known for his ability to prevent planetary disasters.

Now, Reed was restrained with armed guards around him, ready to strike at a moment's notice.

How times have changed.

Upon the morning after being interrogated, Reed was allowed to return to his apartment to pack whatever necessities he needed for his new mission.

Next, Reed was taken to a fighter ship. Standing ten metres tall, it bore the circle sign of the Cosmos Order on both sides, painted in a deep metallic blue. Its sleek design was enough to make any pilot ecstatic.

The Order's ships had revolutionised transportation, granting the government unprecedented speed and economic rise. Both their fighter ships and heavy-duty cargo vessels were engineered to withstand the test of time, with an ensured lifespan of over a hundred generations. The Order invested countless credits and years in perfecting both space manoeuvrability and the consistency of space-way, making even the most obsolete of spacecraft into a reliable vessel.

Reed found it a shame that his destination was so far across the universe. He'd have loved to see this fighter ship in real action. *Perhaps I could use it to escape,* Reed joked to himself, *I'll test before being shot down and crashing into an asteroid.*

Despite the short travel granted by space-way along the countless lengths across star systems, it still proved to make journeys long enough to make the mind drift elsewhere.

If I'm going to find Earth I ought to find out as much as I can.

"Tell me about Earth," Reed spoke to no one specifically. He merely wanted any one of his six guards around him to say something. None of which bothered to share even a look in Reed's direction.

"If I'm going to assist in this investigation, I'll need something to work with." Still, no one responded. "If no one tells me anything, you might as well reroute us to Eion."

Reed cringed at the thought of them doing just that, but he had to get his point across somehow.

"Doctor," The guard across from Reed spoke, "Neither of us knows any more than you do."

"What?" Doyle jerked back as if the ship had suddenly come out of space-way.

Secrets, Reed thought. Did the order want to keep this investigation secure? *Or...had they simply failed to make any progress?*

Reed deducted that it was the second option, as he knew the Order mustn't be succeeding if they required his presence so urgently. Still, he hoped the Order had something for him to work with.

Yes, Reed was considered one of, if not the greatest minds when it came to astrophysics and planetology, but surely the Order would have their own personnel on site.

"What's the Order's take on this?" Reed asked the guard, "Do they have any theories yet?"

There was an awkward shuffling among the seated guards. No one wanted to speak up. Or seemed to have nothing worthwhile to add.

"From what I've heard," a guard hesitated, "the Order is focusing on possible causes of...destruction."

"Destruction?" Reed asked as if the word was an insult to his late mother. "How could they think that an entire planet could be destroyed without a trace?"

"How could they think an entire planet has *vanished* without a trace?" The guard replied, staring blankly at Reed.

Good point, Reed thought. With either possibility, the causes should have been impossible. Or rather, if they had occurred, both should have left a trace or some form of debris for the Order to find.

The distress call of Earth's disappearance had been sent to the Order over one Earth week ago, to which authorities immediately began investigating and searching throughout the known universe.

To Reed's understanding, it was reported as a wild goose chase, leaving countless ships in the empty dark with no hope for results.

The ship slowed almost to a complete halt.

And so I return... Reed stopped his thought, wanting to say *home* before remembering why he was here. His relationship with Earth was the same as most people in the universe, excepting its current inhabitants.

Earth was familiar, a place read about and studied from early ages. It was known for being the foundation of humanity's first struggles and successes as a society and governed system. In many ways, Earth was akin to that of a first child, being that every possible societal mistake had been made and learned from. Of course, the Order would go on to have several additional children before getting things just right to provide a level of consistent stability.

With thousands of years since leaving and expanding past Earth, it had grown to become a grand tourist attraction rather than a residential home world. Additionally, Earth had been transformed into the centre of the Order's industrial hub, with factories, workshops, nuclear plants and shipyards exploiting billions of underpaid workers. These facilities were the backbone for delivering the technological components that fueled the universe's growth.

The planet was one of several thousand currently under the ruling of the Cosmos Order, appearing as insignificant as a single insect. It was easy to reduce a small planet such as Earth to a single number while forgetting that the world was home to over twenty billion people, half of whom were under the control of the Cosmos Order.

The thought of an entire planet, of all the lives on it being reduced to atoms within the vacuum of space, was enough to numb the mind. Such a thing should never occur, not for at least another several million years, when the sun would eventually collide with the Earth. Although being the man Reed was, he knew that such horrors were indeed possible and frighteningly frequent in occurrence.

The ship's back began to open, the shield already on to stop Reed and his armed guards from being sucked out into the dark void. The scenery was always beautiful to Reed, the way planets floated in orbit, how they each tilted on their axes and were all visually unique. But a sinking feeling began to grow inside of Doyle. He could see an empty spot of space in front of him. No moons except the one belonging to Earth were present, and no rubble of any kind could be seen. A space of over forty thousand kilometres by twelve thousand was filled with darkness.

Orbiting around the space, there was life, harboured within four global ships. The ships belonged to the Order; only a government as rich and resourceful as them could ever gather enough funding to design and produce a ship that could stretch to fifty kilometres long and house over half a million.

To see not one but four identical ships, Reed knew this investigation was no joke.

How can they have so much at their disposal and still have nothing to show for it?

The fighter began to approach one of the global ships, drifting towards the side of its shielded docks. Inside the dock, there were transporters, workers, scanning systems, scientists, engineers, practically anyone and anything that was of use for both the ship and the recovery of Earth.

And here I come. One more man to help however I can. It felt idiotic that he was being considered as the missing piece for this investigation, that somehow his work would equate to that of the hundreds of thousands who'd been here for the past week.

It once did, Reed thought. As much as it pained him to confess it, he was considered invaluable.

A sudden wave of hopefulness moved past Reed, filling him with the thought that perhaps all would work out in the next day or two, that the solution to this global catastrophe would reveal itself. Like all waves of emotion, however, it too went away, leaving with it the realisation that this investigation was unlike any other Reed had previously encountered.

The ship finally sunk into the dock, gently colliding with the flooring of the grid reserved only for armed escorts. It was an enticing feeling for the Doctor, experiencing something so similar yet so different in approach. A few years ago, he'd found himself on a similar ship, being dropped off safely for a job involving a planet and a problem that only he could solve. The biggest comparison he found was that he didn't want to be here, and his passion and enjoyment for helping star systems had faded.

Two guards, both of which wore an all-white armoured uniform with a metallic blue circle at their breast, stood on the floor of the bay, waiting for Reed to arrive.

They really mustn't want me to escape. It was understood that Reed was considered a man of value, not to mention an infamous man, but he had to confess that the level of security around him felt too much.

I wonder if I'll be granted a moment's peace while I'm here. Will I have to work with a dozen weapons pointed at me at all times? Or will all my movements be surveyed by the Order?

As Reed began to look at his Artificial Information Multitool, he began to feel a sense of dread for the next however many days he would be working for the Order.

The A.I.M device allowed Reed and anyone associated with the Order to scan the surrounding space, cross-check global communications, and learn just what was occurring at the time of the planet's disappearance. All of this he could find throughout the entirety of the universe, inside the palm of his hand.

Once more, however, the beginning of what sounded like a good lead was killed instantly. The A.I.Ms of everyone throughout the universe were able to be reached, just as long as they were functional, as they were limitless with their contact distance.

But the fact remained that Reed couldn't reach anyone on Earth's area codes.

Too many questions, Reed thought as he began to move towards the global ship.

Too many questions and not enough hope for answers.

CHAPTER THREE

Chain of Command

REED WAS HANDED TO a pair of guards, a welcome change from the previous group, as these two weren't handling any rifles. Reed remained cautious, as he could see the lights of the ship's hallway glisten off each of the guards' reform discs, carefully reminding him who was in charge.

In a fair fight, Reed felt confident he could perform well enough to outmanoeuvre the two guards. He was trained in both astronomical observations and, yes, even simple hand-to-hand combat. But to test himself against a reform disc, let alone two, Reed wasn't willing to take the risk against such transformative weaponry.

Even if he did succeed in beating the guards to a pulp, what then? It was safe to say that the entire ship was being surveyed and that the ones in charge were well aware of the very moment Doctor Doyle arrived. Escaping within an emergency space pod would most likely end up with him being shot down. The same would happen with a fighter ship, knowing full well he wasn't the best pilot.

I really am stuck here.

Reed wasn't sure what to make of his so-called deal with the Cosmos Order. So far, he couldn't make heads or tails about the promises the android had made to him. On the one hand, the Order was known for dealing with past offenders, taking advantage of whatever skills they had and making them useful towards the greater good of the universe. Yet, on the other hand, they showed no mercy towards those who had committed such heinous crimes.

My crimes aren't bad enough to consider that. At least the ones they do know about.

Still, a part of the Cosmos Order was that of good, using its limitless resources and personnel to advance planetary societies.

Reed knew that was certain, at least back when he and the Order were on good terms.

The climate inside of a spaceship always felt odd to Reed. The way it was controlled and had its temperature set always brought him to the point where it felt both too cold and too hot, giving him a weird sensation of shivering perspiration. It felt awfully like the beginning of a fever to him. With that and the odd sensation of artificial gravity, it was more than enough to make Reed nauseous, at least until he became used to it once again.

Of course, his current situation didn't assist in the slightest.

An off-white metallic door, printed with the Cosmos Order's symbol, was raised, revealing the central hall of the ship. From within, there was an amphitheatre stretching around a stage within the very centre.

All seats were taken, revealing a crowd of uniformed people.

Reed stood perfectly still, not in the least ready to meet such an audience. *I thought this would be a little bit more private.*

It was slow at first for the people seated to notice Reed, but once they saw his armed escorts, the entire population of the room turned in his direction.

God, was all Reed could think as he faced the seated people. He turned to their eyes, watching as they stared at him with no emotion. They were all bloodshot, tired and ready to watch their eyelids collapse into slumber. Knowing the Order, everyone here would have been forced to put all their time and effort into finding Earth.

And still, they hadn't. How?

But there was something else Reed saw within the faces of each person before him. Something that made him realise the reality of why he was here, of what he was being brought to do.

They're afraid.

Of course they were. If anyone learned that a planet, a world holding billions of lives, could disappear without a trace...that could cause anyone to tremble.

And now they'll look to me to save it. Reed forced himself to stare straight. The last thing Reed needed was someone to weep and beg him to save Earth.

Reed stood now in front of a grand stage. There were people atop it, dressed in white robes, each with a tattoo of a perfect circle on the middle of their forehead. *The Order,* Reed realised, straightening his back and exhaling his fears.

Reed's guards released his cuffs and left him before not only the members of the Cosmos Order but close to two thousand people.

One of the Order members stood and raised a hand, causing the people to silence themselves. There was no hesitance in the action, nor was there any resistance from those seated.

The robed man spoke, "We come before you all, as members of the second sector of the Cosmos Order to grant everyone the chance to meet our newest aide in the search for Earth." Murmurs were immediately silenced after the man raised his hand once more. "As you have seen and mostly heard, the man before us is Doctor Reed Doyle. A brilliant man from what I have read, and one who possesses a great many skills we require."

Reed felt the need to give a thankful nod to the man. However, it proved embarrassing, as the man failed to see it.

A woman stood now in front of the mass audience. She spoke gently as if everyone before her was her child. "We have all worked tirelessly in the efforts to find Earth. The Order appreciates all the time you have spent thus far and thanks you for your many sacrifices. But there is still work to be done and far more to learn before we can recover what has been lost."

The woman looked down at Reed, staring blankly into his pupils that had shrunken from the bright lights of the room. "Doctor, we, the members of the Order, thank you for coming to assist us." The lady touched her chest and gave a solemn bow.

It's not like I had a choice. Reed's lips tightened as he smiled in reply.

"It is my pleasure, my lady." Reed bowed, "I hope that I will be of some use to you and the Order once again." The lady grinned, probably knowing full well Reed had no such desire to be on board and assisting in the investigation. "Forgive me, but before I begin my work, might I ask you and the Order some questions?"

"Such is your right," the lady answered, "Are they relevant to the planet Earth?"

"Yes," Reed looked around the rows of seats stretching around the room, still uneasy that this wasn't being done somewhere private. "What progress has been made in the last week?"

Both the lady of the Order and the rest of the seated members darted to the person nearest them, waiting for someone to speak. Finally, one of them did. One who looked to be as old as the universe itself.

"So far...there has been no clear indication as to how the Earth could have disappeared or, God forbid, destroyed." Only a few gasps came from the audience.

So no progress has been made after all.

"We have found no sign of debris, no traces in communications after the day of its reported disappearance."

Reed stood there bewildered as to how lacking the Order's results were. They were so lacking that they weren't results at all but instead failed approaches.

"Is that all?" Reed said with a bit too much rise in his voice.

The man who began the grand meeting spoke up, "We have worked *tirelessly* since arriving here, Doctor. Need I remind you that we are trying to recover *billions* of lives."

Lives? Or workers? Reed knew better than to believe the Order was putting such efforts to save people out of the goodness of their hearts. If the loss of Earth was permanent, the Order would need a new planet to declare as their forefront for manufacturing the universe's most-desired resources.

There were several planets similar to Earth, as they held a societal and touristic setting while mainly focusing on resources. However, Earth had proved to be the Order's main source of income. To replace such a planet would cost trillions upon trillions of credits, not to mention several years to accomplish. The Order knew they were better off saving their prime planet rather than creating a new one.

A silence lasted no longer than five complete seconds within the room. Finally, Reed swallowed his need to argue and simply said, "I'll need somewhere to work."

A man stood up from the second lowest row of seats before moving toward the stage. His footsteps echoed loudly, causing Reed to turn.

He was a man of great length, with a well-built proportion, dressed in the same robes as the Order members, however lacking their pure white colour. His skin and robes were completely black, standing with his back straight and chin raised properly. The two things Reed noticed about the man were that he lacked the tattoo on his forehead and that he was rather young, a year or two behind him if he had to guess. Order members were usually fifty or sixty years old; at least, judging from their appearance. Anti-ageing drugs always made it difficult to judge one's age.

"During your stay, you will be taken under the care of Second Premier Whells," The lady among the Order members spoke, addressing the black-robed man now standing next to Reed.

Doyle gave the premier a glance, which he ignored completely. "Doctor Doyle, you will report to Premier Whells, and only him. He is to be you and your team's superior officer during this investigation."

Team? Reed's eyes opened at the word, not expecting such generosities from the Order. "He will also be ensuring that you are doing everything in your power to help regain the planet, and nothing else. I hope you understand."

Work only on finding the Earth and don't attempt any form of escaping, got it? Reed bowed, "I do, thank you, Universal sister, and Universal brothers." Everyone on the stage bowed, the oldest gentleman being the slowest of the group.

"Go forth Doctor, help us bring this planet back to where it belongs," The lady spoke with finality.

The audience let out a short-lived round of applause before standing up and returning to whatever duties needed them. Reed relaxed his shoulders, allowing them to sink as though the artificial gravity was raised just a half of a per cent.

He turned to Second Premier Whells, who still stood sharp, ignoring Reed's existence, until at once he said, "Follow me, prisoner."

What a chipper young man.

Whells walked in front of Reed to what he was guessing to be either his quarters or his workstation. The lights of the global ship hadn't begun to dim just yet, so Reed assumed it was his workstation.

Reed failed to realise just how tired he was from the space-way travel and the comings and goings of his armed escorts and interrogation.

He already knew that Whells would squeeze every drop of work he could out of him. There was something cold about how the man acted even despite how he was so formal in the way he walked, acted and spoke. 'Course Reed had only witnessed the man for a total of ten minutes. There was bound to be room for surprises.

"You look young for your position," Reed attempted to break the ice.

"I am," Whells said with a deep voice.

A few awkward steps passed like a falling comet, "Can you tell me about this team I'll be working with?"

"You'll meet them soon," Whells said, "they're more of a group of verifiers than a team."

"Verifiers?"

"Yes. People who will be ensuring that all your work is relevant and useful to the investigation."

"Excuse me?"

Whells stopped and exhaled. Without warning, the Premier turned around and struck Reed, landing his fist along the Doctor's right cheekbone.

His glasses came off, as did his feet from the ground, causing Reed to land on his backside. Whells moved forward and lifted the Doctor by his coat.

"Now listen to me," Whells said with gritted teeth, "I've read your file. I *know* what kind of man you are, Doyle. Always trying to cut corners and find the easy way out. But here, you will do no such thing. You will work when I say you work, you will do as I say, and you will rest only when I find that you have deserved it. Understood?"

Reed looked at the deep pits of Whells' light blue eyes, only now noticing how much they resembled the blue nebula he'd seen so long ago, currently four-hundred and twenty light years away. He winced as he nodded, knowing full well a bruise was beginning to form on his face. Unfortunately, it wasn't enough to stop Whells from speaking further.

"You may be the expert in this field, but that does not give you the right to command. You will not overrule my orders or disobey me." Reed nodded once more, making it enough for the Premier to let go of him. "I apologise for being stern, but the truth is you are not the only one being watched. We are both under the command of the Order. And I will not allow you to contravene."

If that's being stern, then I'd hate to see him angry.

Whells pulled back his robe, patting down any wrinkles he could find before continuing with Reed. "The Order has placed me in charge of you as... a test to consider my capabilities."

So that's it, Reed thought, rubbing his cheek softly to test the pain. There was a lot.

"For that, I cannot afford to fail nor be embarrassed by your actions, Doctor," Whells mouth grew crooked as he said Reed's title.

"Trust me, I already have enough reason not to fail," Reed said,

The Premier contained a quick laugh, "Then we'll get along nicely."

Chapter Four
Greetings

By the time Reed was brought before his team, his face was lumped, no bigger than a third the size of a golf ball. Unfortunately, the colour of his cheek had already turned into a bright orange, making all the people verifying his work blink twice after a quick stare.

Today, there wasn't going to be any start in the investigation for Reed. That was to begin first thing tomorrow, as Premier Whells so frequently reminded him. All that was to be done for now were introductions.

The so-called 'team' only amounted to a measly four, excluding both Reed and the overseeing Premier; however, Reed was hopeful that each of the members' individualities would prove valuable to the investigation.

As they entered the so-called laboratory, Reed was startled by its equipment. There were deep space scanners, mineral tracers, A.I.M overpasses and a dozen glass screens, all broadcasting a vast expanse of space where Reed knew Earth should have been.

Above the lab's entrance was a timer, increasing with each second from when Earth was reported missing.

Overall, Reed was not impressed by what he saw. But then again, in any other situation, this would all have been enough. The Order would have proved capable of finding Earth, and Reed would have been able to lie in bed and catch up on the latest episode of *Galaxy Conquest*.

Instead, he was here, unsure of how to begin this impossible task.

One step at a time.

The team met Reed one at a time after swarming him with greeting smiles. There was Jessica, an astronomer who studied either on Haple or Laphal, Reed couldn't remember. He'd been distracted after noticing a mask wand by her table. For what reason she had it, he had no idea and chose not to ask.

There was Roy, a rather young physicist looking no older than eighteen or nineteen but was guaranteed to be brilliant no less.

Then there came Pablo, an astrophysicist who came from the eighth colony of Mars as a young man to join the Cosmos Order. Judging from his hushed voice and lack of enthusiasm, he also realised that working under the Order was lacking in benefits and peace of mind. It was draining for Reed to see Pablo as he was, aged and full of regret, but Reed was still proud of himself for making the man smile when he mentioned his love for astrophysics.

Finally, there sat Brandon, who was neither a scientist nor astrophysicist but a cybersecurity consultant. He sat rather too close to the screen in front of him, watching what looked like twenty different A.I.M device recordings all playing at once.

Jessica was kind enough to introduce Reed to him; however, he was only able to produce a rather pathetic nod.

So these are my babysitters.

It was numbing to think of how any work was going to be done in the amount of time Reed would be here. How was he supposed to find a planet if each person here had to crosscheck, verify, and permit Reed's leads?

Something has to be done for me to work properly. At the rate I expect this to go, nothing so much as a deep space scan will arrive when I ask for it.

Everyone, besides Brandon and Whells, was excited to begin working with Doctor Doyle. It was safe to assume they were well aware of Reed's past achievements in terms of saving planets and preventing global catastrophes. Roy especially looked as though he'd met his favourite film star, with the way his hands shook Reed's just that extra three seconds too much.

"We're really, really excited to have you here, Doctor," Roy finally let go of Reed's hand.

"Yes, you said that already," Reed said.

"Oh."

It was a shame that the meeting was so short-lived, as the room and most of the global ship's main rooms' lights began to dim, signalling the start of the ship's sleep cycle. It was common protocol for every ship drifting in space to create a day/night cycle, regardless of whether there was a sun present or not. The point was to create a routine, to ensure there was a cycle of hard work and consistent rest for all present, whether it was for Order members and crew members, and yes, even prisoners forced to work under the threat of extended imprisonment.

Whells gave Reed an unnecessarily powerful shove towards the room's entrance, signalling him that it was time to leave.

Now was the time to show Reed his quarters. At this point, Reed's expectations were as low as the temperatures on Crist. He imagined a cell with no furniture or bed, a shielded container that forced him inside a two-by-two-metre space.

I just hope it's not too hot.

He felt a long stream of sweat pass down his swollen cheek, causing him to wince with stinging pain. From their first encounter, Reed thought nothing but the worst of Second Premier Whells. Sure, the man had more than enough reason to feel anxious while under the trials of the Cosmos Order, not to mention being in charge of a dangerous criminal. Still, Reed felt the need to keep his eye on him, and hopefully not have it obstructed by another swollen cheek.

They arrived not far from the lab; a single door stood in front of them, resembling the countless others that continued down both ways of the accommodation floor.

This looks promising. Reed almost forgot what it was like to have a room all to himself, to breathe and think alone, allowing his mind to finally wrap around this entire situation.

The door opened without a sound of warning, revealing a darkness that could only be found in space. Whells stepped away from the now open door and gestured Reed to enter.

"Your room."

Reed didn't move, unsure of what possible trick Whells was playing on him. The Premier raised his brows with a look that said, 'Well?'

Reed took a step forward, entering the darkened room.

"Sleep well, Doctor," Whells said, flashing a smile so smug, Reed was surprised the Premier wasn't the one with the swollen cheek.

The door shut without warning, separating the Premier and doctor finally. A second passed before the lights picked up Reed's motion.

The room appeared instantly, along with a bed, a desk, Reed's belongings, and even a complimentary fruit basket that held a note saying 'Our many thanks.'

This will do just right. He smiled...for a moment before remembering why he was here, about what brought him here, and what was at risk.

Reed knew he was going to have to work relentlessly.

Reed laid back on his bed, feeling the odd sensation of space drift through him as he sunk into the mattress. He would have most certainly struggled to sleep that first night on board if it weren't for the fact that the last couple of days for him were utterly endless and draining.

He pressed an icepack that he got from the room's freezer against his cheek. The chill of the pack burned him at first but was quickly replaced with a comfortable coolness. As his eyelids began to grow heavy, Reed turned onto his side and asked himself a question. A simple yet impossible question he knew would have to be answered.

How the hell am I supposed to find a planet?

CHAPTER FIVE
A New Day

THE NEXT DAY BEGAN with a blaring sound, screeching so loudly in Reed's ears that he thought there was a breach somewhere in the ship. But the alarm stopped and a voice sounded inside the room.

"Rise and shine, Doctor," Whells' voice spoke through the room's intercom, "We start in fifteen minutes."

With a miniscule amount of enthusiasm and a few self-inflicted slaps to the face, Reed got himself out of bed. Despite the lack of protocol, Reed decided to dress as any astrophysicist would in a professional environment and, better yet, a workplace. He wore a button-up shirt with a pair of loosely fitted jeans and a jacket he knew he'd most likely throw on the back of the chair once he got to work.

Finally, he put on his round spectacles and proceeded to the laboratory.

Everyone had already arrived at the lab. Even the unkind Premier was there, standing tall with a straight back, crossing his arms as soon as he caught sight of Reed.

"Nice of you to join us, Doctor," The Premier said.

Am I late?

"I hope your speed in getting ready for work is not the same when finding leads for Earth," Whells said, "From now on, I expect you to get here before any of your team does. Is that understood?"

Reed looked around, searching the faces of his team members for an answer. Jessica gave Reed a quick shake of the head.

"Yes, sir," Reed bit his lip.

The Premier nodded before placing his arms behind his back and removing himself from the room. The automatic doors closed, and Reed was finally allowed to be alone with his so-called team.

Jessica came to Reed, a look of sincerity spread across her oval-shaped face. "I'm sorry. I should've warned you about him," she said.

"What part? That he throws a good right hand?" Reed unconsciously touched his cheek to see if it was still swollen. It was.

"Ahh, no. Hubert expects everyone to be here at four in the morning. He only ever wakes us up if we've slept in."

"Hubert?"

"Oh, right. I meant Whells, of Course." Jessica leaned over to Reed, "But don't you ever call him that; he hates his first name. Most people just stick to Whells. Or Hugh *if* he's friendly with you."

"I don't think we'll get on that well," Reed confessed, "But thanks for the heads up."

"You're very welcome," Jessica smiled.

"Is there anything else I should know going forward? Is there a dress code? Do I have to stay here until two in the morning or sleep twice a week at my desk?"

"No, no, nothing such as that, Doctor Doyle. Just that you arrive before us, as Hugh said. I usually will get here at around four-thirty myself, so four should work perfectly well for you."

Splendid. Reed knew voicing his complaints in this manner would only make him appear demeaning. After all, what was working such ridiculous hours compared to residing on a planet lost in the universe?

Reed began by approaching each of his coworkers. He needed to see what progress each of them had made and if there was anything to note. It was important for him to know where they held value and what ground they had already covered. If there was any.

"So what do we have so far?" Reed asked. An uncomfortable five seconds of silence passed with Reed eyeing his team, waiting for them to say or do anything. "Have we nothing to show? What have you all been doing the past week?"

"Mostly just routine checks," Jessica was the first to speak, "The Order instructed us to mainly perform scans throughout Earth's area of orbit."

"And?" Reed asked, starting to become frustrated.

"And nothing. Nothing has come up on our scans. No signs of A.I.M signals, no mineral finds, not a single sign of Earth has been found. Remarkably, none of us, nor anyone else on the four global ships has found anything. It's as though the whole planet just vanished."

So it seems. "What about you?" Reed talked directly to Brandon. "What have you found so far?"

Brandon stumbled as if he hadn't expected to be called upon. "So far?" he said with a mouthful of noodles, "Nothing. I've been monitoring media channels, inter-device communications, A.I.M devices, even bloody street cameras, all an hour before the same thing happens."

"Before what happens?"

"Nothing. All devices and systems turn static."

Reed looked away, not wanting to show how his confidence in the investigation was depleting already.

This doesn't make any sense, he thought; *even if everyone and the planet were to somehow move, all A.I.M devices would still be reachable.*

"Okay," Reed exhaled a much-needed breath, "Here's what we're going to do. Brandon, I want you to keep doing what you're doing, look at any surveillance system you can find or think of and watch it for two hours before it cuts out. Note anything you think appropriate. We have to assume that something on Earth was able to record what happened."

"Jessica, Roy and Pablo. I want all three of you to survey what was occurring within the Milky Way galaxy before the planet's disappearance. I want a timeline of everything that was going on. I don't care how small or insignificant it was, whether it was an asteroid blowing past Mars or a ship arriving on Jupiter. I want to know *everything*."

"Ah sir," Roy said with his hand up.

"Doctor," Reed corrected him, "what is it?"

"Sorry Doctor, but what exactly are we looking for?"

"Anything that could have the power to move or remove an entire planet," Reed stated.

"But what could do such a thing?" Roy asked.

"Many things," Reed began, "Space anomalies, black-holes, wormholes, a sudden growth in the sun's temperature or shift in its gravitational pull. Everything, as of now, is a possibility. Nothing here is to be referred to as impossible. Last week, the sudden disappearance of a planet was considered impossible and yet here we are."

And here I am, returning to a life I swore never to see again.

"Doctor," Pablo gained Reed and the team's attention, "what of the satellites orbiting around Earth? Would any of them have been able to see what was happening before the Earth...you know?"

Reed turned to Brandon.

Brandon spun his seat back around towards the group, "I started with analysing the forty-eight satellites when I first arrived here. None of which showed anything peculiar up until the moment of vanishing."

"What about when the Earth did vanish?" Reed asked.

Brandon shifted his office chair back to his desk and began typing, scrolling to whatever he was about to show. "Have a look."

He clicked on a video broadcasted by a satellite that was orbiting in space right above the United States of America. The footage was only ten seconds long but that was enough to send chills down Reed's spine.

The Earth floated as still as a mountain, right where it should have been today. To be accurate, it was supposed to be an additional twenty million kilometres further into its cycle around the sun, being that over a week had passed since the planet's withdrawal. The footage was so still that Reed thought it was paused. That was until the planet...went away, quicker than a blink of an eye.

What came next was a screen that said 'Signal Lost.'

"Roll that back," Doyle ordered, "Slow it to one-tenth the speed."

"Did you see something?" Jessica asked.

"No, but this is the only footage we have of Earth up until it disappeared. Right, Brandon?"

"This and the forty-seven other satellites, yes, however, some are obstructed by asteroid fields, or were positioned in a different direct—."

"Get all of the footage up," Reed cut Brandon off. "I don't care if they show Earth or not; all the footage we have is valuable."

Brandon began his usual routine of clicking and typing at an accelerated rate, flying past an array of documents and archival footage. The whole thing lasted a good half minute before he said, "Ready."

In front of the team now stood a hologram screen, displaying itself against the surface of the ship's protective glass. Reed found it so odd to see footage of Earth play whilst the real planet was nowhere to be seen behind it. All there was on the other side of the window was space. Complete and dark space.

"Slow down all of the footage. I want them synchronised so that—."

"Done," Brandon said with a final click. All of the footage began to play at once, now slowed to an exhausting speed.

Over a minute passed with the recordings appearing as though it was paused, but suddenly, the disappearance occurred. It was just as fast as when the video was played at regular speed, being present within one-tenth of a second and then not.

"Roll it back, frame by frame." Reed could tell his exasperation was getting the better of him. He gripped the back of Brandon's chair tightly and watched the screen he considered had the best view of Earth.

Brandon did as instructed and finally played the footage once more.

It was just what Reed had feared.

The Earth had disappeared without a trace.

Within a single frame, the planet was gone. There wasn't a sound, nor a beam of powerful energy, or anything for that matter that could have pulled off such an impossibility.

What in God's name?

The two single frames played over and over again in front of the team. Reed knew it was pointless but still bothered to look at each piece of the footage displayed. There was nothing, just as much nothing as the other recordings.

"Wait. What happened?" Roy asked, turning at first to Reed and then the rest of the team members. "Where did it go?"

Nobody, not even Reed, answered. They all just stared at the footage, watching it replay.

This doesn't make any sense.

"It seems we have our work cut out for us," Pablo said, breaking the silence, "over a week of investigating and all we know is that whatever happened to Earth, it was no anomaly or foreign weapon nor...anything for that matter."

"But that..." Jessica began, "That's impossible. Planets don't just disappear like that. They just...don't."

"Hate to break it to you, Jess," Pablo stepped forward to one of the screens, "but it looks like that's exactly what happened."

"Jesus," Brandon whispered, almost like he just realised how great of a problem this truly was.

Reed glanced at every one of his team members. He could feel their hopelessness radiate onto him as if they had already decided that they had done all they could.

No. I can't let them give up. I can't give up. Not yet, at least.

"Is there any way this footage could be altered," Doctor Doyle asked no one in particular.

"No," a voice came from behind.

Everyone turned to see Whells standing by the door. Reed remained staring at the footage.

Did it disappear? Or have we been watching a planet, a home for twenty billion people be destroyed over and over? The endless barrage of questions was beginning to ache Reed's skull, more so than Whells' fist.

Suddenly, a theory came to Reed, one he never thought to conjure.

*Could this be...*Reed watched one of the satellites play once again. *Could this be the work of something higher?* Reed never considered himself a man of God, nor did he ever pursue any form of faith despite being exposed to countless religions across the universe. He respected the devotion and commitment beings possessed with their faith, but Reed knew he could never be like them.

He was a man of science, first and foremost, and nothing could change that. Nothing.

But this, only this, made him think of a higher power. Of something with the ability to do the impossible.

We might be working with something beyond the laws of science. Reed leaned back against a wall, trying his best to calm his mind. It didn't help that Whells began to call to him.

"Doctor, might I ask what it is you're doing? Why on Earth are you wasting the Order's time?"

Reed couldn't tell if the Premier meant to say that as a joke or to remind him what it was he was working on. Either way, he wanted to introduce his fist to the man's crotch.

Reed gave the Premier an absurd look, "Excuse me?"

"This," Whells pointed to the series of recordings continuing to replay, "and your orders to survey the Earth as well as the galaxy's timeline before the moment of disappearance. It all seems rather irrelevant, don't you think?"

"I don't think it's irrelevant at all, Premier."

"Wouldn't it be better to pursue our *current* leads? Rather than waste time on—."

"Leads?" Doctor Doyle interjected, "What leads? As far as I'm concerned, I was brought here to help find out what's happened since you and the Order have achieved nothing so far."

"I would remind you, Doctor, that you were brought here because—."

"Because otherwise, I'm a dead man, yes I'm well aware," Reed felt the stares of his team members intensify by the newfound information, "Tell me, can you name any possible way a planet could be destroyed, or better yet just vanish from space? Without taking into account any foreign attackers." Reed knew he could not let the Premier retort. To give him that chance would be sacrificing his queen.

The Premier stood quietly, watching the man he was responsible for continuing to sink himself deeper into an already gaping pit. "No." The Premier's voice fell low.

"No," Reed echoed the answer, "Well, for starters, if Earth were to stray across a wandering black hole's event horizon, then the planet would be swallowed."

"A very unlikely occurrence." The Premier commented.

"True, but it's a possibility. Another possibility is that a wormhole has formed, one that we know not where it leads to or if a second opening has even opened yet."

"The sun itself could have grown to a significantly higher temperature, causing the planet to combust." Reed turned to the array of satellite footage again, "Although

I believe we can rule out that theory judging from this footage and the lack of debris."

Whells looked completely and utterly overwhelmed by Reed's rant. The Premier's eyes began to dart back and forth, searching for a response.

That ought to put him in his place.

"We are not here to waste time, Premier Whells." Reed said calmly, "We are simply ruling out possibilities and im-possibilities. It is slow, yes, but it's a necessary start if we're to move forward and find the answers to this mystery."

The Premier took his time to take in the information. Where his mind was both frustrated and fuelled with em-barrassment, he disguised himself with the same cold look he always seemed to form.

Finally, he presented his back to Reed and said, " As you were," before leaving the lab.

CHAPTER SIX

Days Past

"RUN IT AGAIN," REED rubbed his temple.

"Still nothing," Jessica said after a wide yawn.

Several days had passed since Reed began investigating Earth's disappearance.

Several days had passed and he had nothing to show.

The Earth was still missing and appeared no closer to returning. Despite this, Reed and his team were still proving effective in ruling out possibilities.

The team had created a timeline outlining what exactly occurred the day Earth disappeared. Unfortunately, this proved to tell them anything. Nothing did. Within a week before the Earth's day of disappearance, or D.O.D as Jessica called it, nothing significant or noteworthy had happened. There were some space-way jumps for both business and tourism purposes, some passing debris and asteroids, but nothing too large or close to Earth to be considered a concern.

Why couldn't this have been a solar flare or a nuclear winter? Reed knew that either of those would have been far easier to handle than this.

It was disappointing, depressing even. When anyone in the lab found the strength to speak up and suggest a new approach, they were immediately let down by a logical answer.

"What if the planet is being cloaked?" Roy asked.

For a second, everyone said nothing, almost considering the theory despite it being completely ridiculous.

"We would still be able to contact them," both Reed and Pablo responded. *Great Universe, was this all we were going to do? Bring up theories just to negate them immediately?*

Roy looked down as he sat in his chair, his voice no longer willing to speak up.

"Hey," Reed turned to Roy, "until we find out what happened to Earth, we're going to have to come up with a lot of theories."

"Exactly," Jessica came up beside Roy, gently rubbing his shoulder, "What we are doing is proving what could and *couldn't* have made Earth disappear. The more questions we ask, the closer we are to finding the truth."

For a second, Roy began to smile, nodding as he took in Jessica's words, "You're right."

"Okay," Reed caught the attention of everyone in the lab, "I believe cloaking can be ruled out. But I think we can all agree that if it were truly the case, then this would be a hell of a lot easier."

A chuckle came from both Pablo and Roy. Jessica appeared ready to discuss the next theory.

"Could Earth have been released by the sun's gravitation pull?" She asked.

Pablo began to speak up but was left with an open mouth. "That is actually a good question." He turned to Reed as if expecting him to possess the answer.

"I think this is one for Brandon," Reed said, "Brandon, what can you gather from the A.I.M devices on Earth? Right before the moment of disappearance."

Brandon, after a great many clicks and typing on his holographic keyboard, turned to Reed and the rest of the team. "I've looked at hours and hours of footage, all stretching from minutes to very seconds before Earth disappeared. There is nothing, and I mean nothing, that in-dicates a change in mass or gravity."

Everyone sighed.

Reed had been a part of some challenging investigations in the past, but even then, none could be compared to this. Reed was truly lost and beginning to have his hope dwindle like Earth.

No, Reed protested. *I can't let this beat me, I can't. How will I ever live with myself if I...* He stopped himself, stunned at his thought. Since he'd arrived on the global ship, even when he was arrested, he had only worried about himself. Whether he was going to be gunned by a reform disc or set to Eion for several centuries of imprisonment. Only now, on the verge of defeat, did he realise he was doing this for something other than himself. Mostly.

Reed still would've liked to avoid living on a prison planet for half a millennia.

"Let's take five," Reed declared, "I need myself a coffee before we calibrate another scan."

"I'm with you there," Jessica agreed, "Anyone else want a cuppa?"

Everyone replied with an unsurprising "Yes please." The team hadn't taken a day off since Reed took charge. They hadn't even managed to take a complete eight hours off with Whells supervising. That's not to say the work was challenging or tiring; it was just proving to be consuming as every minute was considered vital. And, of course, the lack of results failed to provide further motivation.

It was almost as though they each stayed up all day and night, working on an extensive report, only to have it be deleted and restarted the next day.

No news or reports of other investigating teams were ever brought up by Whells. When he did decide to visit the lab, he would usually just walk around with his mouth shut and his arms hiding within his blackened robes, ob-serving every little thing the team was working on and looking for any small reason to insult Reed's methods.

Soon enough, he would say something about the lack of results, even if he didn't understand how impossible this task was.

Let me see him try and figure this out.

Whells rushed into the lab, out of breath and with a thick stream of sweat sliding down his head.

What now?

"Everyone," Whells directed the room, taking a couple of deep breaths before continuing, "As you all know, the investigation regarding Earth has so far proved...lacking in its results." For a second, Reed was able to catch just a glimpse of humanity in Whells. The man looked to be genuinely concerned over the planet's condition rather than his career. "Which is why it's been decided to ignore previous pursuits."

"What do you mean?" Reed asked.

"The Order has..." Whells looked almost as though he were ready to faint, but miraculously, he stood tall and strong as ever. "The Order has come to the agreement that Earth... is gone. Destroyed."

Every member of the team looked as though they were slapped across each side of their face. Only a gasp came out of Jessica as she covered her mouth.

"What?" Reed retorted. He couldn't accept this, not without a qualifying amount of proof. And if the last week had accomplished anything, it was that proof was extremely difficult to come by. "Under what principles?"

"The very principles of the Cosmos Order," Whells explained, "They've decided that if Earth was truly missing, it would have reappeared by now. Or that there would at least be some proof to illustrate that its inhabitants were still alive."

"It's been three weeks!" Reed spoke louder than he ever thought he could, shocking himself and the team.

"And in that time you've done nothing but figure out what ships have come and gone in our galaxy and what stars have formed into pretty shapes."

"We've been ruling out possibilities!"

"Possibilities are one thing, Doctor, logic is another. The planet is gone. It saddens me to say it, but it's the truth."

"How can we just rule out that the planet is missing?" Reed asked, looking at all the worksheets and opened files he had on his table and desk screen.

"Because it's ludicrous." Whells snapped, "How could a planet possibility just...vanish?"

"*That* is what we are trying to figure out."

"Not anymore." Whells scanned the room, eyeing everything that appeared to have nothing of relevance to the Order's current agenda.

"From now on, your new assignment is to investigate everything that occurred on the D.O.D. Find out anything about anyone who threatened the planet's safety. And I'm not just talking about Earth, I want all neighbouring planets monitored. I don't care if it is so much as a whisper or a joke; I want to know everything that may be considered relevant. Is that clear?"

The lab was quiet, more than it had ever been since Reed first entered it.

"Is that clear?" Whells repeated.

The team replied with a depressing "Yes sir," to which all their heads fell to the floor. The Premier looked at Reed, who hadn't responded. He was staring at Whells as if he were prey.

"Doctor?" Whells asked.

"So we're spying on other planets now?"

"We're investigating who destroyed Earth. How else are we supposed to find those responsible?"

"By working within the confines of the Space laws," Reed stated.

Whells allowed a quick chuckle to escape him. "Doctor, we are the law. And so are you, by extension, just as long as you continue to work with us."

That stopped Reed from speaking any further. With enough temptation, Reed would've said he no longer was, but he knew better than that. The second he decided he was done, Whells would have stunned him with his reform disc. *Or put a hole in my chest, depending on his mood.*

"Does the Order have any evidence that Earth was destroyed?" Reed asked, already aware of the answer.

"Tell me this, Doctor." Whells walked towards Reed, hands laying behind his back, "What is more possible, for a planet to be destroyed or for a planet to disappear?"

Whells' words came with a point so sharp it stopped Reed from speaking.

How could he counter that? Knowing that destruction was the easier answer, but yet the harder acceptance.

Chapter Seven
New Approaches

THE INVESTIGATION BECAME A splinter that burrowed deep into the minds of the team. It was irritating, knowing that every aspect of their work, whether it involved monitoring a pair of colonial soldiers on Mars or scanning for any signs of nuclear activity, was morally wrong.

With every slight possibility of finding a source that was capable of destroying Earth, Reed whispered to himself, "Impossible." His mind always circled back to how little proof there was.

The Order is wrong. They have to be.

No one in the laboratory said anything, despite knowing that what they were doing was, for one thing, bullshit and another, a waste of resources. Reed could see on every-one's faces that they did not believe in the Order's stance.

But still, they worked. Orders were orders, and despite how incorrect the work was, the team was still expected to provide results.

"Huh," Reed sat up slightly as he finished listening to a conversation from a person's A.I.M device.

"What is it?" Roy asked as he dropped off Reed's third cup of coffee. The warm, welcoming smell made the Doc-tor forget all about how he'd been awake for the last twen-ty-four hours.

"Nothing, it's just...this man, Listil Curts," Reed point-ed to his screen, "He mentions to a coworker that there's a plant towards the western front outside of the city, Crater. But when you look for it," Reed zoomed out of the map of Mars, moving away from a city inside the centre of a large bowl-shaped cavity, stretching over fifty-five kilometres in diameter, "it isn't there."

Roy leaned in to check, "You don't think?"

"I don't know, but the Order will be quick to make assumptions."

Reed considered shutting off the screen, pretending that he hadn't seen it and was mistaken for what it could imply.

Suddenly, a figure came from behind. For a second, Reed thought it was Whells, and began to plan his escape.

"Have you checked it yet for nuclear activity?" Jessica asked, surprising the two.

"No..." Reed answered.

There was a long, awkward stare from Jessica, almost as though she could read what was going on inside Reed's mind, "Doctor, we need to rule out *all* possible causes."

"You can't possibly think the Mars Regime had anything to do with this?"

"I don't," Jessica sighed, "but the Order needs to know. If we do pick up any nuclear levels there, then... then we have a lead."

No. Reed knew exactly how nuclear weapons could affect a planet. They could destroy entire continents and incinerate everything from flesh to concrete. But to destroy a planet to the point of leaving no trace. Not to mention within a twentieth-fifth of a second. No. This couldn't have been done by the Mars Regime, or anyone for that matter.

"Reed?" Jessica spoke.

Reed had his hand ready to perform the scan. It would take only a minute despite how far they currently were from the dry world. "Even if they are hiding nuclear weapons, it wouldn't be enough. A planet the size of Earth would remain even after a million nukes."

"Doctor," Jessica said.

"And if it did destroy it, how could we not know this already? Surely, we would have found what was left of the planet long before even I came here."

"Doctor!" Jessica repeated, finally gaining Reed's attention, "We can't rule out anything. I'm sorry, but you know what Whells said." She touched his shoulder. "I know what you're saying. But we have a job to do. Whatever we find, I'll make sure you have your say. Okay?"

Reed hated to see how the Order got into the minds of its subordinates, convincing them that they were all needed for the good of the universe. *If we were needed, we would still be searching for Earth. But here we are. Spying on anyone we want, trying to find someone to blame.*

Reed tapped his foot, looking back and forth between the screen and Jessica. "Okay."

***

Despite searching for the answer to the wrong question, everyone, including Reed, continued to work for the next couple of days. Everyone would come in early as usual, sit themselves down, and begin where they had left off from the day before.

That was the hardest part. The starting, the way they would each face the same truth every day.

"Nothing," Reed crossed off another name from an extremely long list on his A.I.M. He'd been continuing with surveying random residents of Mars, categorising them into relevant groups that could have possibly been related to any anti-Earth regimes.

Besides his encounter with Listil Curt and the mystery plant he'd talked about, Reed had had very little luck.

"It's almost as if *no one* destroyed Earth," Reed said to himself, although he could tell Pablo heard him from the way he snickered.

"You don't have to convince me otherwise," Pablo said, "I know we won't be able to find anything. At least nothing concrete enough for the Order to take action."

"Then what are we doing?"

"We're buying time."

"For?" Reed asked.

"For anyone the Order intends to blame."

Reed's eyes widened. His first instinct was to deny that the Order would do such a thing, but then again, they were the ones who changed the investigation without a single piece of evidence.

"You know," Pablo began, giving both of his corners a quick look over, "I've been continuing some *previous* theories," he raised his eyebrows, "some more *plausible* theories."

Reed looked around himself, ensuring that no one else was around. He trusted everyone on the team, but he didn't trust them enough to know whether they would snitch to avoid becoming a cellmate with Reed. If they heard Pablo had gone behind the Order's back, who knew how they would react?

"Have you found anything?" Reed asked.

"Shit no, it's just as bad as trying to find people who'd want to harm Earth," Pablo said, "but there is something that's been on my mind lately, Something I can't manage to get out."

Reed listened.

"This investigation, both with how it was before and how it is now. We were looking for the impossible, for things we never thought could ever occur, not for at least another hundred million years."

"Your point?"

"The Order brought us onto this investigation, and ever since, they've acted as though all this was caused willingly. That something or someone wanted to get rid of Earth." Reed's eyes began to brighten with a look. It was the very same look that surfaced whenever the planetologist would begin to think up a theory, a reliable, promising theory he knew would lead to some form of result.

Pablo continued, "But what if...what if this was all an accident?"

Chapter Eight

Cursed Apologies

Accident was such a platitudinous word in this day and age. It was seen everywhere, filling the databanks of everyone's A.I.M devices, describing the same unfortunate circumstances of an event that could have easily been avoided. Whether it was a ship malfunction or a crash between two drivers, people would always describe it as being unintentional. Yet it still caused harm and sometimes even death.

The word accident also translated into something else for Reed. Miscalculation.

It was something every scholar wished to avoid, yet always succeeded in achieving nonetheless. It's because of miscalculation that the universe's strongest minds appeared, for they were the ones strong enough to learn from their errors.

Reed now wondered what great mind was here to mistakenly remove Earth from its galaxy.

Reed began to work on two investigations now. One of which was the same pointless, mind-boggling goose chase that showed no sign of ever concluding.

The second investigation involved researching scientific studies. Reed focused mostly on those found on Earth and paid careful attention to any that appeared large enough to stretch to a global scale.

Reed isolated his A.I.M searches to any scientific studies that were conducted on the D.O.D. Whether they were private or presented in lectures or laboratories, Reed made sure he noted each one.

The only problem Reed found early in his research was that his sample size was far too small. And the only way he would be able to find what he was looking for would be to go back further before the D.O.D.

It was a difficult investigation, to say the least, but it was one Reed was far more confident working on.

Reed began expanding his search by stretching his net to a week before Earth vanished. His main filters for the search were given by the keywords of 'studies,' 'lecture,' 'globally affected,' 'reposition,' and 'scientists.' It was a long shot, but Reed knew it was better than manually checking each case study and cross-checking what it involved.

If everything was right, Reed would find the first real lead.

There was no telling what Reed would find or what horrors he would uncover. He just knew that this was the best chance he had to find answers.

He began the search and leaned back to rub his eyes. It was important to rest his body, especially when looking at nothing but bright screens and floating words for several weeks. It didn't help that when he opened his eyes, he saw Premier Whells standing in front of him.

Reed's body tensed with the expectation of being insulted by the Premier. Instead, he was met with a calming voice.

"Good morning, Doctor."

"Good morning," Reed replied, failing to remember that it was still early.

"I take it everything is going well?”

"As well as can be,” Reed looked over to his monitor, reaching for the shut-off button.

"Please," Whells lifted his hand, “I don't intend on taking much of your time."

"What could I do for you?" Reed retreated his hand from the power button.

"I..." Whells looked around the lab, checking to see if everyone was occupied at their station. “Dammit,” he groaned, “I'm here to apologise."

Reed's eyebrows leapt. “Come again?”

“Don't give me that,” Whells said as if insulted. “Believe me, this is not my choice. The Order members have *encouraged* me to be on friendlier terms with you whilst the investigation continues.”

Reed almost burst out laughing, especially since there was no telling how long this investigation would last. Now that he thought of it, Eion didn't sound completely terrible.

“I thought we were already best buddies,” Reed said with half a smile, although he immediately regretted speaking from the way Whells' face dropped.

"Just be lucky that the Order considers you valuable and so far cooperative. If you weren't either of those, I'd have blasted a hole in you the moment we met."

"Noted. Is there anything else?"

"No."

Then with all due respect, piss off. Reed would have loved nothing more than to say that to the Premier. But then again, he was fond of having an abdomen.

"I'll let you know when I find something." Reed turned back to his monitor.

Whells nodded. "As you were."

He began to leave the lab, slowly walking his way out towards the automatic doors.

Reed breathed a heavy sigh of relief before a robotic voice came from his monitor. *Search complete. There are over twenty-two thousand possible matches from the searches: 'studies,' 'lecture,' 'globally affected,' 'reposition,' and 'scientists' on the planet Earth as of a week before the disappearance.*

Reed winced at the volume of the monitor. He hoped it was only loud because he was the closest to it, but unfortunately, that was not the case.

Everyone began to stare at Reed with wide eyes. Granted, it wasn't because he had gone against the Order's wishes but because they knew Whells had heard it.

Whells rotated around as though he were a planet, slowly orbiting around until he faced his insubordinate.

"Doyle!" Whells cursed.

"Premier, sir, it's not what you think," Pablo interjected, already on his feet and blocking the path between Whells and Reed, "We were tracing back a theory—."

"Get out of my way!" The Premier shoved the man to the side, causing him to fall to the floor. Whells didn't bother checking the man for any injury. All he focused on was Reed.

Reed instinctively raised his hands to surrender, preparing himself to be escorted by the threat of a reform disc, but Whells had no intention of using it. His fists were raised, ready to beat Reed to a pulp.

He wants this to last, Reed thought. The Doctor lowered his hands to the height of his chest, clenching both of them into a pair of tightened fists. *He's not going to be as pleased as last time.*

The Premier exhaled a laugh at Reed's fighting stance.

Suddenly, Whells' right hand swung around in the artificial air, connecting with nothing solid. Reed dashed to the side, standing now behind his opponent. Already, the famous planetologist could feel his back aching, knowing full well that he was out of practice and in need of a dozen muscle adapters.

"I had to do this." Reed spoke to the back of Whells' head, "If I didn't, we'd lose Earth forever!"

"Earth is *gone!*" Whells launched again at the Doctor, only using his arms and legs to tackle him to the ground.

Reed tried his best to block the fury of blows, but his defence immediately shattered after the first hit. His bruised cheek felt like a pinch in comparison to the pain he was feeling now. Over and over, Reed felt the Premier's fists collide with his face, knocking his glasses across the floor.

Finally, he stopped.

Whells' body wheezed with its lack of air, trying to refill his lungs.

"Why...why did you stop?" Reed struggled to speak.

Whells continued to take deep breaths. His fists were still clenched; however, they were badly bruised, possibly fractured by the exchange. "I...I'm not supposed to kill you."

Reed tried his best to laugh but coughed a good chunk of blood instead. "It would be a kindness to do so." The silence that followed was the longest Reed had ever experienced. He couldn't tell if Whells was just exhausted or if he was considering whether or not to finish him.

"Come on, Hubert. You know you want to."

The face Whells made in response was as though every nerve in his body had been touched and severed by a fresh razor blade. He turned ugly, furious as he raised one of his fists, only this time he extended his arm, pointing the clenched hand at Reed. From his swollen eyelids, Reed was only just able to see Whells activating his Reform disc.

The ring around his index finger began to light up, no brighter than a nightlight used for children. Then, the metal basing of the ring moved, splitting to both sides, transforming itself into a divergent shape. The metal extended out, bending into an array of directions and sizes, while the glow of it remained at its centre. Reed could only see the light of the disc at this point, but he knew all too well what was happening.

At least I'll never see the inside of Eion's prison.

Finally, the reform disc stopped in its transformation, now resembling a blaster, sized between the length of a pistol and rifle. It was easily more powerful than both on a colossal scale. Anyone who either worked with or had encountered the forces of the Cosmos Order knew very well a reform disc could produce a plasma blast capable of leaving a two-by-two metre hole in most metals.

The Doctor took one final breath as he heard the weapon warm up.

Reed, the once famous planetologist, a man capable of saving entire worlds, was about to be killed for trying to do the right thing.

If the Earth is truly gone, then perhaps I'll find out soon enough. He closed his eyes and waited for the killing blow to hit.

He felt pain, but not from the disc nor where he expected it to be. It was a pinch, a slight itch at his neck that felt no bigger than an insect. He thought it was just that from the way the sound came with a high-pitched velocity, but the draining feeling of fatigue gave him all the explanation he needed.

A stun dart... Reed turned as much as he could towards the direction of the dart. There, he saw a blurred image, but one that was still readable. *Jessica.* She stood with both of her hands raised, holding the gun.

Slowly, Reed felt his consciousness being sucked away, like oxygen inside the vacuum of space.

Chapter Nine

A Scholar's Cell

Sound, sight, and touch all drifted in and out of Reed's waking mind. He knew he was lying down, whether on a bed or the cold floor of a cell, he couldn't tell. He also knew he wasn't alone. He had visitors, or a visitor from time to time. At first, Reed thought he was being checked by Whells, but the voice he could hear was feminine, higher in pitch, and far more concerned.

"Reed. Can you hear me?"

Leave me be, Reed wanted to say.

The Doctor's mind fell asleep once more, travelling through time at an unconscious rate. There was no telling when he'd wake. A week, a day, a couple of hours? *Perhaps the Earth will be found by the time I wake. But if that's the case, then I am worthless to the Order.*

Reed's heart stung as he completed the thought. As a planetologist, his top priority was the safety of the planets and their people. It shouldn't matter that he needed to be the one to save it, just as long as the planet was returned and unharmed. But he knew if that were to happen in his absence, then he was as good as dead.

Maybe I should just let them take me away. After all, It would prove a great kindness to give me far less than I know I deserve.

"Reed." The voice came again, now clearer, almost as though Reed was finally...

"Jessica?" Reed said between blinking eyes, adjusting to the dim yet blinding light.

"You're awake," Jessica almost cheered, "And alive."

"That tends to happen when you shoot someone with a stun dart."

"Sorry," Jessica's cheeks grew red, "He was going to kill you."

Reed winced as he tried to open his swollen eyes. Despite only being able to squint, he could still recognise that he was inside a holding cell.

"Why am I not dead?"

"Whells thought it would be best to wait for the Order's opinion," Jessica said, "They decided to keep you detained until the mission is complete. Plus, they're not one to waste brilliant minds."

So, Earth is still a no-show.

"So they'll send me to rot, only to bring me back and forth whenever I'm needed." Reed rose from his bed with a stiff back. He didn't even want to imagine how he looked at the moment. Judging from the way Jessica veered back, it wasn't pretty.

"So when am I back in the lab?" Reed asked.

Jessica said nothing, her eyes darting somewhere else in the universe.

"Jessica?"

"You...you're..." Jessica cleared her throat, "Your position in this investigation is no longer active. Whells has decided there is no more for you to do unless it is decided otherwise."

"What?" Reed snapped.

Do they still have any hope left for Earth?

"I tried my best to convince him, but he wouldn't budge. I'm sorry."

"Dammit."

Jessica stood still, looking down at the ground as if searching for the right words.

"What else?" Reed asked.

"They've found them."

"Found who?"

"The ones responsible for Earth."

Reed's head shot up instantly at Jessica. "How?"

"I told them about the scan on Mars, of the unlisted nuclear plant we found." Jessica's shame was slipping out of her lips as they quivered.

"Surely the Order wouldn't believe that the Mars regimes were capable of destroying Earth," Reed said, "They can't be that blind."

"It doesn't matter whether the regimes did or didn't do it. All the evidence points to them. They've always had a personal dislike for Earth and now we know they are capable of bringing destruction to it."

"But not to the point of complete annihilation." Reed added, "The most they could do is reduce all the main continents to a cinder or drain the oceans. Even if they accomplished that, there would still be a planet left to see."

Reed's rows of teeth were scratching against one another. It was beyond ludicrous that this was happening when so many arguments proved it wrong.

"I know Reed, I know." Jessica said, "That's why I'm here." Reed's head cocked to the side, "I can't find the truth about what happened to Earth, nor can the rest of the team. Especially now that Whells is keeping closer surveillance on us." Jessica pulled something from her coat pocket.

An A.I.M device, or better yet, Reed's A.I.M device, along with his glasses. His eyes lit up at the sight, surprised that both appeared undamaged.

"I don't know what you were looking for, Doctor," Jessica said, "But I know it was closer to the truth than anything we've been doing for the last three weeks." She handed Reed his glasses and A.I.M.

Reed put both on. His sight returned with no difficulty, curing most of his disorientation. The rest would have to take time.

A loud banging sounded from behind Jessica, followed by the opening of the shield wall.

"Time's up." The shield came back on, separating the guard from Jessica and Reed.

"I have to go," Jessica said. "Good luck."

"Wait," Reed reached out for Jessica, "If I do find something, it'll be pointless."

"What do you mean?"

"Look at me," Reed motioned to his body and the dried blood stains he currently had on his clothes. "Even if I find who or whatever's responsible for Earth, no one on the Order will ever take me seriously, not now."

"So what do we do?"

Reed paused. It was never wise to not carefully calculate a plan before speaking it, but this would have to be the exception. "You're going to have to break me out."

"What?" Jessica said far too loudly.

Reed gave her a rather harsh shushing. "I don't know how you have to do it, but it's got to be soon. Every minute we waste will bring the Order closer to destroying the Mars colonies."

"How much time do we have?"

"I don't know," Reed was ashamed to say, "It would be best to wait until I find the answers we need. Otherwise, it'll all be pointless."

"Reed," Jessica spoke his name softly, "the longer we wait, the bigger we risk being caught."

"I know. Just...wait for me. I'll call you whenever I'm ready."

"Okay," Jessica said, her voice failing to express any confidence in Reed's plan. She began to leave the room, but just before reaching the shield wall, she turned once more to the Doctor. "I guess we'll both be working on the impossible."

"Not the impossible," Reed said with a smile, "Only the improbable."

Jessica's face grew shocked for a moment before she too smiled. It was clear from the first day the two met that she knew just who Doctor Reed Doyle was and what he had done for planets and civilisations. But it was only after hearing the smallest reply of optimism from him that she understood what made Reed so special.

***

It was challenging to conduct an investigation alone, especially now that Reed's company consisted of only armed guards. They would visit him every two to three hours, carrying a fresh tray of food and drinks, including a bottle of medicinal syrup and an orange drink rich in vitamins and minerals.

They must want me to be strong enough to travel through space-way; Reed noticed the increasing dosages; *why else would they want me in top shape?*

What also made the investigation challenging was the fact that it was lacking in leads.

Jessica had done the kindness of uploading Reed's search results onto his A.I.M device. From there, he needed to check every result that came up in relevance, starting with lectures that were live either on the D.O.D or within a week prior. At times it became increasingly tempting to search further before the D.O.D, but Reed knew that would end in an endless pursuit.

Additionally, Reed couldn't shake the feeling that he was wasting his time when discovering such promising scholars. In his endless search for answers, he found a great many people he would have loved to have met and converse with. One of the scientists he saw was presenting a lecture at The University of New York, where he showcased an invention that could convert an atom's subatomic particles.

The Order would've recruited him in a heartbeat. Reed saved the lecture in his record library.

If I'm lucky, I'll be able to meet this man one day.

For what felt like days, Reed stared at nothing but his A.I.M device, hoping that an answer would reveal itself.

A banging came from the shield wall, causing Reed to remove his A.I.M device from his wrist and hide it under what scraps of clothing he had left on him.

So soon, Reed thought, hoping that whoever was coming wasn't Jessica. He was nowhere close to escaping just yet.

The static sounds of plasma were removed as the shield wall collapsed, revealing Whells.

The Premier gave Reed a quick look from head to toe, shaking his head at what was left of the planetologist. Reed kept his eyes fixated on Whells before noticing he wasn't wearing any reform discs.

That's somewhat calming, Reed thought, knowing his life wouldn't be taken from him just yet.

Whells stepped past the shield wall border and nodded to a guard to activate it. He did, and now both Doctor Doyle and the Premier were alone once again.

"How are you feeling?" Whells asked.

"Excuse me?"

"I said, how are you feeling?"

"Better," Reed replied.

He hummed as if disappointed, "You're to be taken to Eion by the end of the week."

Reed's heart collapsed like a supernova. He sighed, "You must be thrilled to be rid of me."

"It's not what I would have chosen for you, but then again, I'm in no position to question the will of the Order." Whells' shoulders sunk within the comforts of his robes.

Reed began to eat the last of his food from the tray, which consisted of beef strips layered with rice and soy sauce. Not an exciting meal, but one Reed appreciated, especially in his current situation. He wasn't feeling at all hungry; truly he was stuffed, but the news of being sent to Eion with such short notice...well, it would be foolish to waste such a meal.

After all, on a planet where death was a myth, food wasn't a necessity.

"Why did you disobey me?" Whells asked.

Reed paused at that, unsure whether the truth would land him in even more trouble if that were even possible. "I did what I did because there was nowhere else to turn. I've studied star systems, galaxies, space anomalies and all the rest since I was a kid. I've..." He stopped himself, afraid that he'd confess his most critical failure. "I've seen almost every possibility in terms of planetary disasters. But this...none of this makes any sense. Nothing should be able to cause a planet to just...disappear."

Whells absorbed the words one by one, "Let me offer you a piece of advice, Doctor." Whells took a step forward with his arms wrapped around his back, "In my years of working for the Order, I, too, have seen almost everything. I've witnessed rebellions rise and fall within an hour, and I've seen economic collapses be averted right before the point of disaster. I've even watched a planet be consumed by its core."

Reed gulped at the mention of a lost planet. The occurrence of such a thing was rare, of course, but in recent years, it was hard to ignore that the number of lost systems has risen to a concerning number.

Does he know? No, how could he? Only I was there to witness it. To survive it.

Whells continued, "And when I was told how each of them occurred, I learned one thing," Whells stared at Reed with his blue eyes, "Not everything requires a reason or a clever answer; sometimes, things just happen."

"Well, I'm afraid that's just not good enough for me."

Whells coughed a laugh, "When I was told I would be supervising you, I read everything I could. Field reports, agent logs, and even some of your own accountings. I truly thought the reports on you were exaggerated, but my, how you live up to your reputation." Whells glanced at the Doctor, not with anger or frustration. He was admiring the planetologist.

"You should be the one standing here," Whells said, "I don't come anywhere close to your level of experience."

"Then why did you take this assignment?" Reed asked, genuinely curious.

"I wanted to serve my leaders. Prove to them that I was capable of charging a team to do the impossible."

"And do you feel you've accomplished that?"

"I do. We now know who was responsible for destroying Earth, and soon enough, they will be brought to justice."

Reed shook his head, "Whells, it wasn't the Mars colonies."

"It *was* them."

"How can you be so sure? What evidence do you have?" Reed asked.

"The very same you provided us."

Reed felt a stab at his chest, stopping it from beating for a full second. He sighed, "That doesn't mean it was them. Other planets in the universe have been known to possess hidden nuclear activities."

"Have these planets held agendas against Earth for the last hundred years?" Whells gave Reed a smug expression. "And are they also positioned adjacent to Earth?"

Reed remained silent, knowing full well it was useless to argue with a man as stubborn as Hubert Whells. Any cocky or outlandish response to him would surely make Reed regret it later.

"I'll let you know when we've completed our mission, Doctor."

"Whells," Reed called out to the Premier, now making his way out of the cell room.

He hummed, waiting for whatever Reed had to say.

"You said I should be in your place. That you're not the right man for the job. Then why do you choose to ignore my advice?"

"Honestly," Whells said, "because I know I'm right. As does the Order."

"How lucky that you took the job," Reed said, "I'm sure everyone will be thankful that you were up for the task after you and the Order eradicate the Mars colonies."

"It won't be eradication. It'll be justice." Whells snapped back.

"Will it be justice knowing the man you've sent away could've saved Earth?"

"You twist my words, Doctor. I didn't say I couldn't complete this task. I only said you held more qualifications than me." The Premier signalled the guard to close the shield wall, "I'll confess, being put in charge of this investigation was an experiment for the Order. But, with the work you and your team have done, it's proved to be quite a successful one, don't you think?" The Premier gave Reed one last look. "Safe travels, Doctor."

Reed watched as the Premier's dark robes were replaced with the shield wall's bright blue light.

None of this makes sense. Reed considered what Whells had said, about how this all had a simple answer to it. *No. Nothing about this is simple. There has to be a reason this all occurred.* He tossed and turned as he lay down on his bed, contemplating all the theories he conjured and proved wrong. *Where could have I made a mistake?*

Accidents, Reed recalled his current approach to the investigation. He hated to admit it but at this rate, it was leading nowhere. *No. There is still a chance I can find the answer. Isn't there?*

In the hypothetical sense, it was more reasonable for the condition of Earth to be that of a purposeful act rather than being unintentional. *How could such a thing occur, regardless of motivation? How could a planet just...*

Reed sprang from his bed.

The word echoed inside Reed's mind as he recalled Whells saying it. Finally, the Premier was proving to be useful, just when it was the most inconvenient.

This has all been the result of an experiment. The most detrimental experiment since the testing of the first atomic bomb. Reed covered his mouth with shaking hands.

Only now did the silence of Reed's holding cell become aware to him. It filled him with a chilling fear, knowing but not knowing completely that what he was theorising was the truth behind Earth. And only he knew about it. Only he would be able to figure out the truth before it was too late.

***

It was ludicrous the amount of work one could accomplish when sleep was taken out of the equation. Reed couldn't afford to waste time to recover; such time was worth more now than the diamond rains of Neptune.

Normally, such a thing would prove almost impossible for Doctor Doyle, knowing full well his limit for staying up was between twenty to twenty-two hours, depending on how strong his coffee was. Luckily, he was being supplied with a great number of medicinal syrups.

The guards would return soon after Reed took the powerful medicine, collecting the empty vials he had emptied. They were strict about when the syrup was to be ingested and that Reed was having the correct dosage. Having too much or too little of the syrup could easily cripple the body's healing system, causing Reed to be unfit for space-way for another month.

Where the cell guards weren't strict, however, was with food. They understood the needs of one's body and the fluctuating appetite prison life could have on a person. For that, they allowed Reed to keep whatever food he was given throughout the day, including bread.

The frequent meal trays always arrived every few hours throughout the ship's day cycle, arriving with a form of protein, some vegetables, and a roll of bread. The guards became used to Reed keeping his bread, making it last him a good hour after receiving his newest meal, as well as his medicine.

The taste of syrup-soaked bread was even more displeasing and awful than Reed imagined. The first couple of days, he struggled to hide how awful the syrup's bitterness ruined the bread's floury texture. But it proved worthwhile, for Reed was able to work and concentrate for several consecutive days.

This'll end terribly for me, Reed dreaded the near future of when he'll inevitably be forced to stop the dangerous ingestion of the healing drug, for it brought terrible withdrawals.

But it didn't matter. Nothing did except the answers.

Many hours were wasted with potential leads. Some appeared promising, some were so outlandish that Reed thought there was the off chance it was the one he'd been searching for for so long. They all brought Reed back to where he began.

Even with the medicinal syrups that not only healed his body but greatly improved his overall morale, Reed couldn't help but feel the shadowing dread of defeat lurking behind him.

But that was until he found just what he'd been looking for.

Chapter Ten
Hypothesis

THE 'EXPERIMENT' REED FOUND was a lecture, consisting of an almost empty audience.

At its centre, there was a man. Worn with experience but with the voice of a young scholar, he stood, waiting to address those who'd come. His name, as he often repeated, was Professor Issac Dowensky. He paused after he said 'Professor,' as if it would help capture the audience's attention.

It didn't. If anything it only succeeded in making the audience regret how they were spending their afternoon.

The Professor began to draw on a screenboard and ramble about movement and the limits of modern transportation. He complained about space-way and the drawbacks it brought with it, explaining that it was an unnecessary strain on precious resources.

"From an economical viewpoint, space-way will lead to a Universal disaster," Professor Dowensky drew an 'x' across the words 'Space-way.'

He has a point there.

Doctor Doyle's eyes watered as he forced himself to watch. The lecture had been going for over an hour now, far too long for Reed to continue without any signs of promise.

That is until, finally, the Professor captured both Reed's and the audience's attention.

"It is from these objections to the current state of our universe that I propose a new way of transportation. A way that will make *entire* civilisations move across galaxies...within a nanosecond."

Reed cocked his head at the intriguing yet concerning proposition. It sounded even more farfetched due to the man's thick accent; however, Reed watched on.

A woman came from behind the stage, holding something as large as her torso, draped in a thick white cloth. Professor Dowensky pointed at the object. "Behold, ladies and gentlemen," he said as the object was placed on a desk beside him, "the future of transportation."

A sudden, yet hesitant clapping came from the attendants. Their eyes were fixated on the object, waiting for it to be revealed.

The Professor pulled the cloth.

An onslaught of gasps rose from the audience. The device, now in complete view, resembled an hourglass, standing a foot and a half tall with a widened middle section. Rather than being made of glass, it was made of a solid dark metal. And instead of holding sand, it held something else entirely.

All the faces within the lecture room seemed as confused as Reed. The material in the middle of the device looked to be neither solid, liquid, nor gas. It was a dark, deep spiral of purple, constantly moving in a circular pattern, appearing as though it was growing and shrinking while remaining the same size.

"What you are about to see is merely a prototype; however, I believe that it will showcase its capabilities nonetheless," Dowensky said.

The woman moved towards the device with a tennis ball in hand.

Dowensky gestured to the woman, "My assistant is about to demonstrate how exactly this device works and how it can perform the extraordinary." The woman raised the tennis ball, rotating it so that all could see. "What you see here is a tennis ball. It has not been meddled with, nor enhanced in any way."

Professor Issac Dowensky pulled out what appeared to be a remote controller, "My assistant will now throw the ball into the centre of the device. From then, we will see it reappear ten feet away, instantly." The professor nodded to his assistant, giving her the go-ahead.

Dowensky's assistant pulled her arm back. To miss the device would be a crushing embarrassment not only to her but to Dowensky as well. She breathed, steadying her nerves, before hurling the ball towards the device. The ball met it spot-on and then... the ball disappeared.

Gasps resounded throughout the room. Unfortunately, they disappeared quicker than the ball. Seconds passed, then minutes.

Nothing came back from the device, nor within ten feet of it.

"This was a waste of time!" One of the audience members said.

"Where's the ball?"

"How come it didn't come back?"

"My friends, please." Dowensky pleaded. This is merely a prototype. If you'll just—."

"You said it didn't matter!"

The audience rose from their seats and began to file out of the auditorium.

The recording ended, freezing on Professor Dowensky's flushed face and burning eyes.

Reed did nothing but stare at his A.I.M, taking in what he had just watched.

Is this what I've been after all along? Reed asked himself. *Did this man continue his experiments to the point that it was capable of making Earth disappear?*

He rewinded the recording, watching the moment the ball hit the purple material of the device. He slowed it down to a single frame, noticing how it resembled the speed of Earth disappearing.

At the moment of impact, the ball vanished, failing to reappear. Only now, the recording in front of Reed revealed something. A trace. A single fuzz of fibre floated from the device and drifted in the air before landing on the desk.

Reed looked at the trace with a weary eye. He began to theorise about what had happened between this experiment and the day of Earth's disappearance. The recording of the lecture was from a week the D.O.D. *How much progress could Dowensky have made in such little time?*

It was ludicrous to consider that the Professor would have been able to enhance his prototype since the lecture, but then again, since Reed began this investigation, almost everything was beginning to look all the more possible.

Reed's mind was numb. He'd been awake for several days now, doing nothing but watching lectures and experiments, hoping to find answers. It was a surprise that he hadn't passed out already.

So many of Reed's searches were completely irrelevant, holding no common factors with the investigation of Earth.

Is this truly what I've been looking for? Or am I just clinging to hope?

Reed decided then what he had to do. If he was wrong, he'd have wasted valuable time.

He clicked replay on the lecture and leaned in with a sharp eye.

***

The lecture ended once again after over an hour. There were moments when Reed wanted to shut the damn thing off and move on to the next lecture he had lined up. But finally, Reed came to a hypothesis. One that both intrigued and terrified him.

He was making a teleportation device, Reed realised, never imagining such a device to be crafted. Being a man of science himself, the argument of relocating objects was always heavily discussed.

Many scientists at some stage in their careers explored the concept of pursuing the impossible, such as exploring parallel realities, developing a perfect artificial intelligence, or delving into another's subconscious.

All of these ideas were brought up during Reed's studies. It was a way of allowing the mind to become creative while also forcing it to be critical in the laws of physics and reality. He recalled several times how he had to explain how instant relocation or teleportation, as it was commonly referred to, couldn't work.

It was all because matter couldn't pass through matter.

But from what Reed was seeing, both from the lecture and the Earth's satellite footage, teleportation could have finally been cracked.

To move anything within the blink of an eye, a ball, a ship, a planet...

Reed's body shivered as he stared at Dowensky's face. He knew who was responsible for Earth's disappearance. The pieces were finally aligning, but still, Reed had so many questions.

To start, Reed could tell Professor Dowensky's device had been improved since his lecture; a man having so much to say would not let a failure end his attempt to help the Universe.

But there was still the issue of the trace. The tennis ball in the demonstration had left a trace, and yet Earth hadn't.

If Earth had left a trace, just as the ball had, then the Cosmos Order would have found it easily.

And I would be back on Haple, living my life peacefully.

The next part to consider, if the Earth had indeed been teleported, was why it hadn't returned. And why hadn't the ball returned either? The device might have destroyed them both, but why had only the ball left a trace?

Could it have teleported into a sun? Reed horrified himself with such a question. *No, no. Even that would have given us some form of debris.*

Reed sighed, grateful that he could eliminate that possibility. *Why did the ball leave a trace?*

The remote control, Reed eyed the device as he skimmed through the lecture. *He calibrated it to reappear ten feet away, but he didn't specify in what direction.* Everyone assumed it would return within the direction of Professor Dowensky or his assistant, but nobody ever thought it would return from above or...

"It did return!" Reed's voice echoed inside his empty cell. *So why hasn't Earth? The Order has searched almost everywhere in the universe, and we still haven't been able to make contact.*

With every answer came another dead end. Reed wished he had his team with him now. Having them here would allow him to finally rest and let someone else think for a while.

He laughed at the thought of being able to teleport them all here. To ask them what they thought of this outrageously improbable theory before teleporting them back would be a wonder to witness.

If the device still didn't work, there's no telling what could have happened. Such an unstable device could cause mayhem. The smallest miscalculation could...could... Reed's eyes widened. His hands began to tremble as he shut off his A.I.M.

"Earth is still teleporting," His voice broke, "over and over and over again, throughout the lengths of the universe."

Dowensky succeeded, Reed realised; he made an entire civilisation travel across galaxies.

Chapter Eleven
Breaking Point

THE NEXT FEW HOURS were some of the longest for Reed. He had so much information within him and so many questions, he could not rest until he knew the answers.

The sound of closing plasma brought Reed's attention away from the depths of his overrun mind. There, at the entrance of the cell, was Jessica, along with a young man Reed knew he should've recognised.

"Roy?" Reed turned his head at the young physicist, his eyes still marvelling at the site of Doctor Doyle.

"Hello, Doctor," Roy said.

"We got your message," Jessica said, "You have the answers?"

"Most of them," Reed said, "I'll be able to find the rest once I'm out of here."

"Are you sure you'll be able to save the planet? Because once you're out, they'll hunt you down," Jessica warned.

"I am," Even Reed was shocked to believe himself. For the last few weeks, he was beginning to think he'd never find Earth or the answers to what had caused its disappearance.

Finally, things were starting to make sense, mostly.

"Okay," Jessica pulled a mask wand from her pocket and directed it at Reed. "Stay still please." A light shined from the tip of the metallic wand and began to scan Reed's face. "So what's the plan?" Jessica continued as though she was conducting a chore.

"Ah..." Reed hesitated just as Jessica began to scan Roy's face. His reaction wasn't quite as stunned as Reed's.

"Go on," Jessica insisted.

"I found someone who may have teleported Earth." Reed's words sounded ridiculous even to himself.

Jessica froze, "Did you just say teleported?" Roy asked.

"Yes," Reed said.

"How is that possible?" Jessica asked.

"I don't know." *I wish I did.*

"So does that mean Earth has just been somewhere else in the universe this whole time?" Jessica asked.

"Yes, and no," Reed watched as Roy and Jessica became even more confused. "My theory at the moment is that Earth is instantaneously moving from different points in space throughout the cosmos."

Both Roy's and Jessica's mouths proceeded to journey to the floor.

"But that...it doesn't..." Jessica failed to comprehend such a phenomenon.

"I know. The whole thing still makes very little sense to me, but nothing else seems remotely plausible."

"Was there anything else you found?" Roy asked.

"No, only that," Reed confessed.

"So what are you supposed to do then? Find this Professor and beat the answers out of him?" Jessica began scanning Roy's face again.

"He was on Earth," Reed revealed, "Getting to him will be impossible." The light from Jessica's wand retreated into the tip, and after came a sound, signalling its completion. "The only way to get answers will be to find his assistant."

"His assistant?" Jessica asked.

"Yes. His sister, Victoria. At the time of Earth's disappearance, she was, and still is, on Second Jupiter."

"Reckon she'll have the answers you need?" Jessica asked.

"I hope so," Reed said, "She has to. Otherwise, Earth is gone, forever."

Jessica surveyed her mask wand, "Well, we better get moving then," she said right before shooting her metallic stick at Reed, and then Roy immediately after. The wand sent a layer of white light, blinding them both for a mere moment.

"Reed, I need you to panic. Act as if you've just been attacked." Jessica said, "Roy, you know what to do."

"Yes ma'am," Reed knew it was Roy who spoke, but his voice was different, familiar. Almost like it was his own. Then he saw who was in front of him, standing next to Jessica. It was himself, a perfect replica of what he looked like.

"What the hell have you done?" Reed asked. He touched his throat, confused as to why it sounded so squeaky and young.

Am I...Roy?

"I've given us a way out." Jessica said, "Now call the guards."

"What?"

"Call. The. Guards."

Reed did as he was told. It was so strange to yell with the voice of Roy and the young muscles the man had in his facial structure. "Guards! Guards!"

Roy, now resembling Reed, began to grab Jessica, wrapping his arms firmly around her neck.

"What are you doing?" Reed asked.

"Getting you out of here," Jessica said. The adrenaline of the affair was too much for Reed to think, that and the hours upon hours of unrest he forced himself to work through. But finally, just as the guards entered, he understood what was occurring.

"Guards! Help! He broke out and threw me in here!" Reed screamed the words to lengths his body would've struggled to produce.

"How the hell?" One of the guards spoke.

"Get back, or I'll kill her," Roy said, pretending to put pressure on Jessica's neck. The guards didn't listen.

They began to move closer to Roy, pointing their reform discs directly at him. Reed could tell they were ones made for stunning. Roy must've known too, as he didn't seem all that concerned.

Does my face always look like that when I'm tense?

One of the guards shot at Roy, avoiding Jessica entirely. He jerked back before loosening his grip on Jessica and fell against the cell wall.

"Good shot," the other guard said, his reform disc still pointed at Roy's unconscious body. "How the hell did he get out?"

"We don't know," Reed said, "He just snuck up on me and threw me in here."

"Endless universe," The guard cursed, "The Order is always cutting costs on the things that matter. Come on, let's get you out of there." The guard waved Reed to the entrance of the cell before opening it. Just as quickly as they let Reed out, they put Roy inside, leaving him there unconscious.

The people of Earth will owe him a great deal of thanks.

"You two better get out of here," The guard said, "best you go back to your quarters and rest up."

"We will. Thank you." Jessica said, "Come on, Roy." It took Reed a second to react to that name.

The two left the cell room and proceeded down the ship's hall. Jessica leaned over to Reed, "We have to move quickly; the facial cloak won't last for long."

Reed nodded and followed Jessica down the hallway.

***

"We're here," Jessica said as they entered the hangar bay, "See that ship over there?" She pointed to a small transporter.

"That ours?" Reed asked.

Jessica nodded, "I asked Whells if Roy and I could leave to check out a possible lead on Mars. He didn't even ask for specifics; he just gave us the go-ahead."

"That man is as dense as he is stern." Reed shook his head.

How long will it take before that man causes disaster?

"Let's get moving," Jessica said.

The hangar bay was just as busy as the day Reed arrived on the Global ship. Dozens of workers, dressed in white uniforms, bustled around him. They were transporting supplies, performing maintenance checks on shuttles, and overseeing the comings and goings of spacecraft.

How long will we have before someone notices us? Reed eyed the station workers and patrol guards.

They continued onward and stood before the transporter. "Get in," Jessica said.

Reed entered the ship, standing atop the ship's stairs. Jessica remained outside, gazing up at Reed. "I already uploaded a route to Second Jupiter on the nav system. You'll have to put in a more specific destination yourself."

"You're not coming?" Reed asked. He could feel his voice slowly changing back.

"I can't. Roy will look like himself soon. I've got to make sure they don't do anything to him."

"You'll be imprisoned, Jess."

"I know," Jessica lowered her head, "But if that means we have the slightest chance of finding Earth, then—."

Without a whisper of warning, a sharp plasma blast assailed Reed's ears, followed by a bright blue light, temporarily blinding him. The world went white, swirling in and out of focus.

"Reed?" Jessica's voice called. Reed opened his eyes, his vision returning slowly to normal.

Oh no.

Jessica stood at the bottom of the ship, now with a gaping hole around her chest. The flesh around the wound was already cauterised, preventing any blood from gushing out.

Reed could tell from the blankness in Jessica's eyes that she was dead. She collapsed, revealing the killer behind her.

Whells, Reed wanted to curse the man; no, he wanted to launch himself at the Premier and strike him with all the strength he could muster. But not now. He couldn't allow himself to sacrifice his life just yet.

Reed hit the button to the right of him, causing the ship's stairway to close, removing the sight of Whells and Jessica's corpse.

I'm sorry. Reed fought off the coming grief. Now was not the time.

Plasma blasts came from Whells' reform disc, echoing against the ship's interior. There came other blasts, re-inforcements Whells had probably called for. Reed was going to have to move fast if he ever hoped to escape the Global ship.

Reed ran to the cockpit before starting the ship and initialising his route to Second Jupiter.

"Come on, come on, come on!" he said to the controls.

"Doctor Doyle!" Whells' voice came from the ship's communication speaker, "I'm only going to say this once. Exit the ship and turn yourself in. I have twenty rifles pointed at you."

Reed activated the speaker on his end, "Where was that warning for Jessica?"

"She knew the consequences of treason," Whells said, "Plus, she wasn't as valuable an asset as you are. The Order would demote me if they knew I didn't ask you to surrender before killing you."

"You son of a bitch," Reed spat out the insult, "you and everyone in the Order are fools. Can't you see that we are dealing with something other than political agendas?"

"No," Whells spoke with a single note, "you are the one who's blind. You've plagued everyone here into believing your ill theories when the very answers have been right in front of you."

Reed knew he couldn't argue with a man like Whells. The only way to stop him was to bring Earth back.

"Come down, Doctor. Help us bring those responsible to justice. There's still a chance that I can make a deal with the Order." Whells spoke like a businessman now, trying to make a sale even though Reed wasn't buying.

The ship rose several metres from the station floor, hovering like an asteroid with no destination in mind. Finally, Reed pulled on the ship's hydraulics and began to fly out of the station. Whells and the rest of his guards were shot back by the thrust of the ship's engine.

Reed couldn't help but smile. To feel a ship like this in his hands was a rare luxury, but one that would have to be rushed.

"So long, Premier," Reed cut off the communication speaker.

Reed flew out of the hangar. Normally, he would wait until there was a clear enough path before jumping into space-way, but there was no time. Any moment, a dozen star-fighters would come from each Global ship and begin firing at Reed until he was reduced to rubble.

Reed had to leave now. He had to get to Second Jupiter as fast as he could.

Reed positioned the ship away from any obstacles he could see and pressed the ship's space-way activation.

Within the blink of an eye, Reed and his ship were gone, disappearing into nothing but stars and space.

Chapter Twelve
Over a Drink

Second Jupiter appeared as quickly as the Global ship vanished.

Reed was entering into the marble planet's orbit, unsure of what region he would land on.

Let's hope the cosmos lands me where I need to be. Reed didn't want to imagine how terrible the possibility would be if he were to land on the opposite side of the planet. He was short on time. Even shorter now that the Order was aware he had escaped.

They would eventually find him. It was just a matter of when.

As the ship made its descent, Reed searched for Victoria Downesky's location. According to Reed's A.I.M, Victoria had recently changed her residency to Second Jupiter and was now living in the downtown part of the city, Dusk.

That will have to do for now, Reed prepared a guide to that very location and was awed when he found that the ship's nav system had brought him to that very area.

If Jessica were here and still alive, he'd have kissed her for her brilliance.

Instead, he was alone. Reed closed his eyes before wiping a single tear from his cheek. "Thank you," he said.

***

Doctor Doyle began journeying along the downtown parts of Dusk. He brought up his A.I.M and displayed a profile shot of Victoria's face. He gazed at the people he passed along the streets, hoping that the woman would magically appear. She didn't.

Normally, Reed would ask the police for assistance but with his current situation, there were just as many stars as there were reasons not to do that.

Time passed with a lack of results and a few odd stares here and there. Reed considered the possibility of finding other acquaintances of Professor Dowensky; however, the chances of them understanding or even knowing of his teleportation device's existence were slim to none.

A beaming light of neon glowed against Reed's face. He turned to it and saw a bar sign with a martini being poured into a glass and the words 'Come in?' The sight made his mouth watery and caused his body to sink. Reed couldn't remember the last time he'd had a strong drink, nor anything that wasn't medicine or full of vitamins. With the start of his withdrawals beginning to sting, Reed knew he couldn't say no to the sign.

Plus it would be very nice to sit down for a change.

Reed entered the bar. The place looked like it had been refurbished recently, with a nice front bar free of stains, and a collection of unopened bottles behind it. It was a shame that the only people occupying the venue were an older couple, a trio of what looked like cargo carriers, and of course, the bartender.

"What can I get you?" The bartender asked.

Reed sat at the front bar. "Brandy please," he answered.

"On the way, sir." The bartender said with a smile.

Reed looked at his A.I.M as he waited. He'd been looking at the lecture again, trying to see if anyone might have met with Dowensky afterwards.

Even if anyone did, they were likely to be on Earth at the time.

The bartender came back quickly with a bottle of brandy and an empty glass. She poured the amber liquid slowly, "What brings you here at this time of day?"

"What do you mean?"

She laughed as she finished pouring, "Guess that makes you an off-worlder, considering you didn't realise that right now it's about four o'clock in the morning on Earth."

"Oh," Reed gave a fake laugh.

"Trust me, there's no use in hiding. People like you tend to stick out like a sore thumb." The bartender smiled. She slid the glass towards Reed. "So where you from?"

"Nowhere close. And nowhere far."

"A secretive man. How intriguing. Can I ask what brings you to Second Jupiter?" she asked.

Reed felt that telling the bartender the truth was of no use, but then again, how badly could it hurt to mention it?

"I'm looking for someone," Reed welcomed the brandy, taking a generous sip.

"Oh? Anyone specific?"

Reed brought up the picture of Victoria, "I'm after her."

The bartender's eyes widened at the sight, "What do you want with her?"

"I just need to ask her some questions," Reed said.

A silence roamed between the two. Reed kept his eyes fixed on the bartender, unsure of what it was that he'd done to make her stand so still.

Does she know her? he began to theorise, *No. She could've just lied and let me go on my way. Why is she...?*

Suddenly, with lightning speed, a blaster appeared in the bartender's hand, aimed directly at Reed's forehead. Reed failed to react in time, his body spasmed from the unexpected rush of adrenaline.

"Easy," Reed raised his arms slowly.

"What do you want with Victoria Dowensky?" The bartender spoke as though she'd rehearsed the line.

"You know her?" Reed asked. His head only just cocking to the side enough so that the woman wouldn't think he was trying to attack.

"I'm not going to ask you again," The bartender cocked the blaster, emitting a sound of produced energy.

"I need her help," Reed knew it was best not to lie to the woman, considering the size of the blaster and her twitchy forefinger, "and so do the people of Earth."

"What?" the bartender looked at Reed as if he'd said the dumbest thing.

"I need to talk to her about her brother."

"What does that have to do with Earth?"

Reed swallowed, unsure whether she'd believe him after what he was going to say, "I think he caused Earth's disappearance."

The bartender's face twisted. She looked ready to pull the trigger but instead lowered her arm.

"Dammit," she holstered the blaster, "What has my brother done now?"

***

Reed still couldn't believe how different Victoria looked compared to the screen capture he had. On his A.I.M, Victoria had blonde hair and possessed a rosy face that held a pair of sharp cheekbones. Now, her hair was short and dyed a dark red, and her lashes were coated in a thick layer of mascara. Reed couldn't tell which look he preferred.

Reed and Victoria moved to one of the booths after she had ordered everyone out and declared that the bar was closed.

She poured herself a drink, "After the lecture, I couldn't take it anymore. Always doing what he told me, cleaning up his messes. I had to get away. So I left. I found this place and started living a new life."

"You've done well, considering the lecture was only over a month ago."

"It could do with a few more customers," she glanced around the bar.

"Victoria, I need to ask you some things about your brother."

She took a large gulp of her drink, causing Reed's brows to rise. "Go ahead," she said.

"What was he working on?"

Victoria laughed before treating herself to another drink. "I don't know. He never told me what it was. I may be his sister, but to him, I was only his assistant."

Reed nodded, not wanting to push on the subject of their relationship. "He said something about wanting to transport entire civilisations," he said.

Victoria hummed, "He was...obsessed with our home world after it had been destroyed. He couldn't stop explaining how he could save everyone. And our parents."

"You're not originally from Earth?"

Victoria shook her head, "No. When we came to Earth, he spent all his time and what was left of our inheritance on...I don't even know."

"So what does the device have to do with your home world?"

"I have no idea. Perhaps it was a madness that came from grief; who knows?" Victoria finished the rest of her drink with a large gulp, to which Reed moved back with awe, "So you think whatever he made has somehow destroyed Earth?"

"No. I believe your brother invented teleportation."

Victoria's face became stupified, "Teleportation? But that means..."

"It means he made an error and now he's removed the planet and himself from the Milky Way galaxy."

Victoria's brows were raised for a good ten seconds, trying her best to comprehend what Reed had just said. Hell, she probably needed another drink.

"So...where did he...where did Earth go?"

"I don't know," Reed began, "But I do have an idea. If what he has is merely a prototype, then the device is unstable. I'm only theorising here, but my best guess is that he's somehow made it so Earth is in a constant redirection from one area of space to the next."

"You mean...Earth, as we speak, could be teleporting across the universe?"

Reed nodded, "I believe so."

What was initially shock was now fear on Victoria's face. *She really had no idea.* She stared into nothing, probably looking back on all she did with her brother.

"Victoria. Victoria," Reed had to raise his voice.

The woman shook her head as if remembering where she was. "Sorry."

Reed sighed, "I need to know if there were any dead switches, any protocols, or something that could deactivate the device?"

Victoria's eyes flicked rapidly from left to right, "I don't know. I didn't even know what the device was until now."

"Please. Think."

"I honestly don't know," she shook her head.

Reed leaned back in his seat. *After all this. The one good lead, all for this.*

"Doctor?" Victoria said.

Reed let out a groan.

"Why do you assume Earth is constantly teleporting?"

"All communications from Earth have failed to reach the Order, or anyone in the universe for that matter. If they had only been teleported to one point in space, then we'd be able to reach them."

"But what if they've lost power?"

Reed's head shot up. He stared at Victoria with a curious eye, "What do you mean?"

Victoria leaned forward, despite having the entire room to herself and Reed, "Years ago, we did a test, back when *it* was only a small contraption, no bigger than an A.I.M device. We thought we were successful, but then it happened."

"What happened?"

"We lost power. As did everyone else within a ten-mile radius."

"Did it ever come back on?"

"Only after we and those affected had their power supplies replaced."

Reed sat quietly for a while, contemplating this new information. To think that Earth could be somewhere in the universe without power, without a way of contacting the Order. Surely, it couldn't have been that simple, yet so inconceivable.

"So Earth could just be somewhere without power?" Reed loathed the idea, but he would gladly accept it if it was the answer.

Victoria nodded, "We fixed the bug as we progressed in size and scale, but Issac could've easily made a mistake along the way."

"You think a bigger device would have the power to cause a global blackout?" Reed asked, "The one I saw was only about a foot tall. How could a device that small be capable of that?"

"That wasn't the only device we had," Victoria said as though it were obvious.

"What?"

"We used *that* device for our demonstrations. But the *real* one was back home, bigger than this very building."

Oh, was all Reed could think. "So where would Earth have been teleported to?" Reed finally asked.

"I don't know. Unless..."

"Unless?" Reed repeated

"It's a long shot."

"I'll take anything."

Victoria's eyes began to water, her voice shaking, "At the edge of the universe, in the Toric Galaxy."

"Why there?" Reed asked.

"That's where Issac and I used to live. Our planet resided there before the war reduced it to rubble."

That could have been another reason why Earth's location hadn't been found yet. The Toric universe had been abandoned ever since its capital planet was destroyed by war, or so the records told.

But Reed knew the real reason for the planet's annihilation, a reason that still haunted him at night, leaving him to question how he could've prevented such a disaster.

"I'm sorry," Reed said with almost as much grief as Victoria. Reed cleared his throat, trying his best not to get distracted. "So Issac teleported Earth there as a way to...what? Bring back his home world?"

"As crazy as it sounds, I think that's exactly what he intended."

"Instead, he may have doomed another."

Victoria wiped her eyes, "So what now?"

Reed stood up from his seat, "I have to go. I'll find Earth, inform the Order, and hope it's not too late to save everyone."

"And return Earth to where it belongs," Victoria added.

"Yeah," Reed didn't know how that part was going to play out. There was no guarantee that Earth would ever return to its original place, at least not any time soon.

"Thank you, Victoria, for everything." Reed offered her his hand, to which she accepted, "Just promise me this, Doctor. Stop my brother. And make him understand that nothing can bring our home back."

"I will," Reed promised, tightening his grip.

***

Reed returned to his ship with a depressed speed. He needed the time to think things over, and more importantly, to grieve, now that he knew the terrible truth.

When he finally returned, he sealed himself inside and allowed his body to mourn for the first time since that day. The day he had destroyed a planet.

It's all my fault, the planetologist confessed; *all of this is because of me.*

Chapter Thirteen
Orbiting Past

Space-way always allowed the mind to drift. Whether it was from the silence of space or the endless drifts of stars ahead, it always gave a person the time to sit and reflect. For Reed, he could only think of the past and how it had shaped the present.

After all these years, I'm finally returning.

Reed hadn't returned to the Toric galaxy since that day. Why would he? There was nothing to see now except rubble and an area that once populated over seventeen billion souls.

"Theef," Reed whispered the planet's name, not knowing the last time it had left his lips. The neighbours of Theef consisted of dwarf planets, populating no more than a few hundred million each. After the destruction of Theef, everyone had been forced to flee the galaxy.

Reed was probably the only soul within 50,000 parsecs.

The core was supposed to be stabilising. Reed thought back to when Theef's planetary makeup was under threat of rapid decay. He thought he could prevent it. He thought...

The fact that a war was on the verge of starting made the world's destruction less relevant to Reed's presence. When the planet's plates began to shift and crumble the surface's landscape, everyone believed it was due to atomic weaponry. No one ever suspected that it was the great Doctor Reed Doyle, the man who'd saved countless planets. And destroyed only one.

If only..., Reed sank his face into his hands, feeling the endless agony of Theef's destruction. He'd help save a great many people that day, but when so many billions died, it made no difference.

In a way, Reed couldn't blame Professor Dowensky for what he'd attempted. Anyone who'd lost their home would have done anything to bring it back. Whether it was a house, a family, or their entire planet, they deserved to have it returned.

But Reed knew he couldn't allow Dowensky to succeed or even fail should it cause the people of Earth to die.

Perhaps if I saved more lives that day, all of this could have been avoided. A failure such as Reed's was enough to make him mad, to cause him to endlessly question what he could've done differently. But the past couldn't be changed, and those who'd perished couldn't be brought back.

There were only a couple minutes left until Reed reached the Toric galaxy. It was enough time to change his course and contact the Order. Reed would have to find a haven quickly, somewhere the Order's reach was weak. Reed began searching for somewhere fitting that criterion while also bringing up Whells' contact.

They can handle the rest from here. Reed had his finger on his A.I.M, ready to call the Premier.

Reed looked up before he tapped on 'connect.' He watched as the stars in front of him drifted into an endless light, beaming with no start or end. It was one of the many sights Reed always cherished during his travels. It was only after Theef, that such moments became rare.

No, I can't run away from this. Not again. The planetologist shut off both devices, keeping the ship's course on entering the galaxy. He had to see Earth, he had to know that he was right and that the Order wouldn't attack Mars.

The space-way journey was coming to an end, pulling Reed back into the pilot's chair with a powerful force. Reed took control of the ship, knowing full well this area was populated by asteroid fields. Immediately, a gigantic rock, ten times the size of the ship, came hurtling towards him. Reed evaded the asteroid, only to find another, far smaller one in front of him.

He spun the ship, ducking and shifting away from all obstacles before finding a clear patch of space.

He initialised a space scan, deep enough that it would monitor and find all planets and large masses of matter. Reed assumed Earth would now be residing exactly where Theef had years ago, but then again, that was assuming Dowensky's device had teleported it correctly. The scan was going to take a few minutes. Reed continued to fly towards Theef's location at the centre of the galaxy.

By the time Reed arrived at the location, the scan was complete, leaving him completely disorientated.

"It's not here." Reed's breath left him like he was in the vacuum of space. He scanned the galaxy again, staring at where Earth should have been.

Could I be mistaken? Reed asked himself, *Wasn't this where Theef once was?* He checked his A.I.M for Theef's planetary records, hoping its coordinates were different to where Reed was.

He was in the right place, and yet there was no sign of life anywhere.

Earth was not in the Toric galaxy, just as Theef wasn't any longer. He slammed his fist onto the ship's control console. "This doesn't make any sense!" he groaned, both from the pain and the realisation of his failure.

"Doctor Doyle." A voice came from the ship's communication system. Immediately, a dozen fighter ships came into view, weapon systems armed and pointing at Reed.

Reed eyed the ship's controls. He liked the idea of dying in a desperate escape rather than living a thousand-year sentence.

"Stand down. We have you surrounded, Doctor. Now explain yourself," The officer said.

"Isn't it obvious?" Reed asked sarcastically, "I came here to hide."

"The Order thinks otherwise. They require your presence."

Before Reed could respond or begin his escape, the closest fighter shot a beam of dark, transparent light towards the ship, pulling him into a gravitational pull. The ship was paralysed, shutting down all systems except the air, gravity and communications.

"Hang tight in there. We'll have you back before you know it."

Reed collapsed and watched as he was pulled back to the Milky Way galaxy.

Chapter Fourteen
Order and Mayhem

Reed was ushered into the Global ship's council room, where the members of the Cosmos Order awaited. Despite all that had happened, Reed was glad that he was given a private meeting this time. He wasn't sure that he could withstand another public audience.

Although the council room was excessively spacious, it lacked the seating platform of the amphitheatre, making for a more comfortable experience for Reed. It also helped that this room offered a captivating view of the galaxy.

All that was missing now, was Earth.

"Doctor Doyle," the eldest of the order members spoke, "you were brought here with the chance to eliminate your list of crimes. But from what I've seen, you have only suc-ceeded in increasing it. Please, explain yourself."

"And what crimes are those exactly?" Reed was fully aware of what they were, but he wanted the man to say it out loud.

"You have disobeyed your commander. You have con-tradicted a Second Premier on multiple occasions, and finally, you escaped custody and attempted to contact the Mars colonies."

That's new. "Excuse me?" Reed said with insult, "I did no such thing."

"To which crime do you deny?" The woman among the order members asked.

All of them, Reed struggled to swallow those words. "I did *not* attempt to contact the Mars colonies. Why would I travel to the Toric galaxy?"

"To avoid surveillance and capture from us, of course." Another member spoke, "Had you travelled to Mars, we would have contacted our spies immediately."

"Well, with all due respect, you're all mistaken," Reed said.

"Then what were you doing in such a desolate place?" The woman asked.

Reed sighed, unsure of how the members would take this. "I was there to find Earth."

Silence echoed within the room.

"The planet is gone, doctor," a member said, "destroyed, never to be seen again."

Reed considered the possibility. If Earth hadn't been transported to where Theef was and still hadn't been found, then perhaps Dowensky's experiment *did* destroy the planet.

But still, something told Reed that that was not the case. There was still something he'd missed.

"It can't be gone," Reed whispered.

"You said so yourself that you went to the Toric galaxy to find Earth." The member said, "From what I've heard the planet wasn't there. Unless there is something we are not aware of."

Reed lowered his head, ashamed at the fact that Earth was nowhere to be seen within the Toric galaxy. "No. Earth wasn't there."

Chuckles came from all but one member. "What made you think Earth was there?" The voice belonged to the only woman among the members. Even now her voice was calm and comforting despite all that was happening.

"I had a lead," Reed said, unsure whether he should reveal all that he knew about Dowensky and his teleportation device.

"Could you elaborate, please?" The member asked.

Reed panned to the other members of the Order. He noticed then that Whells was standing at the back of the room.

Reed took in a deep breath. He didn't know whether it was better to tell them all he'd found or to remain silent.

But what good would it do? he thought. *It all led to nothing in the end.* Reed's gaze narrowed on Whells, his fists clenching as he remembered all the harm the man had caused. And of all the harm he was going to cause.

Reed sighed. They needed to know, on the off chance that it could stop the destruction of the Mars regimes. At least then Reed could still save one planet today.

Reed told his story about how he stumbled upon the Professor's demonstration of his range of theorising, followed by his questioning with Victoria Dowensky. All had seemed to intrigue the Order members; however, it all seemed to dim as they knew it led to a lack of results.

"But if Earth wasn't there, then where is it?" One of the members asked.

"I don't know," Reed said.

After that, there came a solemn silence, a moment that seemed to honour the memory of those who had perished on Earth.

"It is a shame that no result came from your investigation, Doctor Doyle," the oldest member spoke, "as much as we would like to believe this, there is still a lack of evidence. Evidence that we have otherwise found by examining the Mars regimes."

"We wish to avoid conflict with them," Another member spoke before Reed had the chance, "but the fact is that they are responsible for destroying Earth. For killing billions of innocent lives."

And billions of workers, a spark of anger flickered inside Reed. He hid it before making one last demand of the Order. "All I would ask is that you give me more time. Please, I know the answer is out there somewhere."

"We admire your efforts, Doctor Doyle, but the fact of the matter is that Mars is an enemy of the Cosmos Order." The oldest member said, "And it will soon be eliminated."

A sudden vibration charged its way through the floor of the room. The ship was turning, moving away from Earth's area of space.

Reed's eyes were locked on the glass screen. He watched and waited as the reddish-yellow planet of Mars came slowly into view.

Before the Cosmos Order, Mars had been a vast desert world, empty of life and resources. But for the last millennia, the world was transformed. Some still considered it a barren land, but that didn't hide the fact that the planet held lush patches of greenery and vegetation that sprouted to the most unlikely of crevices.

Reed never thought much of the planet. Whenever he was met with the sight, his mind returned to his early years of study and research.

But now, knowing what was about to occur, Reed couldn't help but notice the beauty of the world.

Fighter ships began exiting from the global space crafts. There must have been thousands upon thousands of them flying towards the planet, all armed with atomics, ready to kill those who were reported as enemies of the Order.

Reed didn't know to what extent that was; from the reports the Order had been given, he wouldn't be surprised if the entirety of the planet was considered hostile. Regardless, a great many lives, both innocent and guilty, were about to be lost.

"Whells, please!" Reed turned to the Premier. The man's breath fogged against the glass screen as he watched the beginning of the assault, "Stop this!"

"Why?" Whells asked, "This was your doing." He smiled at the desperate planetologist, "You helped us find the ones responsible. Now we can watch them be brought to justice."

This isn't justice. This is genocide.

The ships were on the verge of entering the planet's border. Their weapons were armed and awaiting commands.

Suddenly, a great shot of light came from the planet, blinding Reed and everyone in the room.

Damn them all to hell. Reed kept his eyes shut. He knew if he opened them he would only be able to see Theef. The way the planet had shattered into trillions upon trillions of pieces made Reed want to die.

He failed then. How was he supposed to face another failure now?

I'm sorry.

Reed's eyes began to recover. He blinked before turning towards the glass panel, awaiting the horror of Mars's destruction.

But something was off.

The light Reed assumed to be the first wave of explosives did not resemble any atomic he'd seen before. Upon deployment, atomics left a cloud of dark black, mixed with a fiery reddish orange.

But from where Reed was, he could only see a deep purple. And It was coming from the side, away from Mars and the fighters.

"What the hell was that?" one of the Order members barked into his A.I.M, "Was that the regime?"

Before Reed could react, he had Premier Whells marching towards him, his hand ready to clasp around Reed's throat. "What did you do?"

"Sir," a panicked voice came from the A.I.M, "there's been no response from the regime."

"What's our ship's status?" The member asked.

"The ship is perfectly fine, sir. But there's been—." The voice cut out before returning with an ambience of rejoicing.

"What the hell is going—."

"Sir! It's Earth. It's back!" The A.I.M cut again.

"What?" Everyone in the room said the same thing.

The ship turned to the left, away from the direction of Mars, back towards where the global ships had been for the last month.

The turning of the ship was the longest experience in Reed's life. A part of him was doubtful that the planet had returned miraculously without explanation. But another part was hopeful, desperate even to believe that what he had just heard was true. Reed closed his eyes. He waited and waited until he opened them as the ship became still.

There she was.

Mother Earth was positioned exactly where it had been thirty days ago. Its bright blue light made Reed's eyes water, almost as if he was staring at a lover he hadn't seen in a great many years.

How?

Reed spun towards Whells and the Order members. Each of their mouths was open, although Whells' looked to be about an inch away from the floor.

"Stop the assault," Reed ordered as though he were a captain of a platoon.

One of the members tapped at their chair's A.I.M and said, "Hold off on the assault. Fall back to your GS stations and await further orders."

"Was this your doing, Doctor?" Another member asked Reed.

"No, my lady. But I think I know whose it was."

"As do I." The lady said. She tapped at her A.I.M, "Have a ship prepared with a strike team for Doctor Doyle and Premier Whells."

"Yes, my lady," The voice on the other end of the system said, "To what destination?"

"Earth."

Chapter Fifteen

A Man and His Creation

THE HANGAR BAY WAS in a state of panic. Med-wings were leaving five at a time. Alerts were constantly calling and requesting crews to be ready. And here Reed was, standing beside Whells, waiting for his transport to Earth.

Among the swarming crowd, there came a group of soldiers. They were covered from head to toe in black armour, moving with almost no resistance, while carrying a rifle that could make Reed's arms cramp. Twenty of them came before Premier Whells. Their backs straightened in perfect synchronicity before making a crisp salute.

They mustn't want to take any chances, Reed thought, now that the Order was finally believing his theory.

Reed didn't know what to expect of seeing Dowensky in the flesh, nor of the device's current state. Reed only knew that he had to find him before he could run another test. And after Issac was arrested, Reed would shut the machine down, forever.

They entered the transport and took off from the hangar bay.

Reed began searching the Earth's residential files, now that Earth's live records were being uploaded to everyone's A.I.M devices.

"Tell me something, Doctor," Whells said, "if the earth wasn't destroyed, and if it wasn't transported to where Theef once laid, why has it all of a sudden returned?"

Now he asks for my advice, Reed couldn't help but imagine taking one of the soldier's weapons and using it on Whells' smug expression.

It *was* a fair question, one that Reed wished he had the answer for, but he did not reply. The bastard didn't deserve one. He didn't deserve anything except being sent to Eion.

"Doctor?" Whells said.

Reed remained quiet. He didn't trust whatever words would come out of him.

"You and I both know I didn't have a choice. From what I had, Mars was the only possible cause of Earth's destruction. If you were in my position, you would have done the very same."

I would have listened to those I assigned. I would have asked questions. Helped where I could. I would have done anything in my power to save them. I would have...

The explosion of Theef flashed in front of Reed. Billions of lives gone within the blink of an eye, and all that was left was a man.

"No," Reed whispered.

"Excuse me?"

"I would have done nothing like you. Nothing at all."

Whells smirked, "Come now, Doctor. Don't let grief cloud—."

"This isn't about grief," Reed snapped, "this is about you failing as a leader. Because of you, the universe almost lost another planet."

For once, Whells' face became a blank canvas, conveying no emotion of anger or remorse or even joy. He just sat and stared at Reed, listening to everything the man had to say.

Reed continued, "It's because of people like you that the universe is in disarray."

Whells looked at all of the soldiers sitting with him. They had been listening, waiting for his reaction. They must have all been disappointed as the only thing Whells did was sigh and say, "We'll be arriving shortly."

***

Dowensky was living in the states, just twenty miles south of the main industrial region. Even though Reed knew of Earth's current reputation in the cosmos, he couldn't help but shake his head at the sight of Earth.

Where life stretched to the bright colours of green and blue, now there was only darkness, made up of smoke and ash.

The ship landed only a block away from Dowensky's residence; from there, Reed, Whells and their strike team began to move.

They arrived outside of Issac's home. The team surrounded the perimeter, checking each window for any sign of Dowensky or potential dangers.

"Clear," came a voice from across the house.

Reed sighed. He stepped forward and knocked on the front door with a polite touch. No one answered, nor did explosives or boobytraps, as some predicted, trigger.

"Allow me, doctor." Whells brushed past Reed. He stared at the door, before unleashing a solid kick. The lock shattered with a crack, leaving the door hanging crookedly from its hinges.

Reed rolled his eyes. "Well, that worked."

The strike team began to slowly search the house. The floors creaked as they moved with precision. They held their rifles high across each space, fingers resting on the triggers.

While the team was at work, Reed and Whells waited in the kitchen.

The place was quite clean for a man who reportedly lived alone. There were no piles of dishes in the sink nor layers of dust by the window sills. There was a picture by the bench table framed in a smooth, dark wood. The picture was of a planet, of Theef, appearing as beautiful and lively as the first time Reed had seen it.

Reed placed his hands on each side of the frame before lifting it.

A click sounded and then a sharp scraping of stone echoed within the house.

"Sir," one of the soldiers entered the kitchen, "a door opened in the study."

Whells looked to Reed, nodding as if to say, "Good work."

Reed looked away. He proceeded to the study, to which everyone, including Whells, followed.

The sound of generating electricity reverberated from within the depths of the concealed door. Reed entered, not knowing how deep underground the pathway went or where it led to.

As Reed descended an endless spiral of stairs, he could feel a surge of energy flow within him, tingling his skin. The hair on his head and body began to rise and fall like waves, making him all the more confident that this was the right place.

He continued, leaving a small gap between Whells and himself.

A purple light began to shine from the end of the walkway, flowing as if it were reflecting a great pool of water.

He moved in closer and closer before coming to a clearing. *What on Earth?*

Reed's eyes fell on what he thought was the device from Dowensky's lecture. But this was far too big to be a prototype.

The machine was at least thirty feet tall, looking completely identical to the prototype Reed was familiar with. Only now the purple spiral was even more captivating, almost hypnotic, as if there was no greater sight in the universe.

It was only because of a man standing in front of the machine that Reed was able to snap out of his trance.

"Dowensky," Reed whispered, looking now at the professor who'd done the impossible.

"Good lord," Whells said as he entered the room.

Below them was Issac Dowensky, scribbling an equation on a whiteboard almost as wide as the device.

"Professor Dowensky!" Whells called out. The Professor stopped writing and turned towards Whells and Reed. His face was unchanged.

"I thought I had more time." Dowensky said, "But I guess I miscalculated yet again."

"Professor Issac Dowensky," Whells signalled the guards to follow him towards the Professor, "In the name of the Cosmos Order, I, the Second Premier Hubert Whells, place you under arrest for the crime of endangering the safety of Earth and its people."

The professor cocked his head, squinting at the Premier as his hands were already laid out willingly. "Did you just say Hubert?"

"Professor," Reed spoke, "I'm sorry for what happened to your planet. But taking Earth won't bring it back."

The Professor's face continued to twist as his eyes darted from Reed to Whells and finally to his machine. Dowensky closed his eyes and began to chuckle before sucking in a warm breath of air. "How interesting."

Reed felt a chill crawl up his spine. *Why is he so relaxed?*

Whells finally came within gripping distance of the Professor. He wrapped Downesky's hands with a pair of handcuffs, closing them tightly despite the man not appearing as a threat.

Reed kept his eyes fixed on Dowensky's body, waiting for some concealed weapon to reveal itself. He watched and waited but saw nothing from him. Everything felt wrong. *Why isn't he resisting?*

"Your residence, your belongings and most importantly, your machine are now the property of the Cosmos Order." Whells escorted the Professor out of the room. "When the investigation is completed and it is deemed safe, your laboratory will be seized, your research will be captured and your machine will be destroyed. No further harm will be caused by your unsupervised research."

"No!" Dowensky's relaxed nature was now replaced with uncontrollable panic. He struggled with the grips of Whells and his men, wriggling about like a caught fish as he cursed them on. Reed remained where he was, watching as the scene took place.

"You can't do this!" Dowensky yelled, "It's my home. I have to go home. No!"

Before long, the strike team was able to get Downesky out of the lab. But Reed could still hear his screams.

Before Reed followed, he looked one last time at the machine, at its gorgeous purple spiral, folding and unfolding in an infinite surge of energy. He leaned forward, eyeing the Professor's stack of papers and written equations.

I could understand so much more if...

Reed saw the Premier at the corner of his eye, his finger hovering atop his reform disc.

"Doctor," Whells said, "The Order awaits us."

Reed sighed, knowing his job was complete. He nodded and began to return to the ship.

I still don't understand, Reed hated to admit. There was still so much he didn't know. So much he still didn't understand. *Why was there still a piece missing from this godforsaken puzzle?*

He scanned each room he passed, taking every detail he could. Reed thought of everything he had witnessed throughout the last month. Thinking and rethinking until his mind grew numb.

There has to be an answer to this. There has to be.

Reed entered the transport, not knowing if he'd ever return here. *They'll burn it all before understanding what they stopped.*

As the transport lifted into the air, Reed gave Dowensky's home one last look.

Home. I have to go home.

Chapter Sixteen

Answers

Reed stood idly as Whells made his report in the council room. At this point, Reed wanted nothing but to sit and quieten his thoughts.

"Professor Dowensky was preparing for another test when we arrived at his lab," Whells explained to the Order members.

"So there is no doubt that this was what caused Earth to vanish?" One of the members asked.

"Yes," Whells answered, "Dowensky didn't deny his crimes when we began questioning him. In addition, he was expecting us."

"Why?" Another member asked.

Whells' failed to respond. He turned to Reed and motioned for him to speak.

Reed was dazed in his thoughts. The world was muffled in a constant blur.

Reed shook his head, remembering where he was and who he was standing before.

"There is no definite answer as to why he was expecting our arrival. Of course, If it were up to me, I'd wager that he was expecting to be arrested *after* he succeeded."

Let's hope they believe this, Reed eyed the members of the Order.

"Succeeded?" One of the members asked.

"Dowensky intended to relocate, or in this case, teleport Earth, to the Toric galaxy, specifically to where Theef once laid," Reed could feel his palms begin to sweat, "Upon succeeding, I believe the Professor would have begun to destroy his machine and prevent us from ever moving Earth back to its original place."

"So that's why he was confused." Whells looked at Reed with wonder, "He thought we were in the Toric galaxy. He thought he'd won."

"Precisely," Reed said, "We should consider ourselves lucky that he didn't complete the calculations for his machine."

"I'm sorry Doctor, and Premier," The oldest of the Order interrupted, "But if Earth didn't relocate to the Toric galaxy, and Earth wasn't destroyed, then why was it gone for such a period?"

"That is a fair question, sir," another member commented, "We've questioned our fellow members of Earth and they've said only a few hours have passed for them."

"It's simple really," Reed bit his lip. He had to lie to them. There was no way they could know the truth.

If they knew what I knew, there would be no doubt that the Order would exploit it.

"As impressive as Professor Dowensky's device is...was, it was still a prototype. An advanced prototype, but not the machine he intended to create. If Earth wasn't relocated to the Toric galaxy, and if it wasn't destroyed, then there is only one other explanation." Reed wished he could tell the truth, just for the moment of witnessing everyone's reactions to the unthinkable possibility. But he didn't. Instead, he gave a false yet mathematically and astronomically viable answer. One that he knew they would believe.

"The planet *was* teleported. But not once, nor even a handful of times." Everyone stared at Reed, waiting for his hypothesis. "Throughout the last month, Earth was in a constant state of relocation."

Everyone digested Reed's words, processing them in complete silence.

"Go on, Doctor," one of the members spoke.

Reed checked his A.I.M, "For us, the planet was gone for a total of thirty days, two hours and sixteen minutes. But for everyone on Earth, it all happened within a fraction of a second."

"But how can that be?" A member asked.

"Speed." Whells said.

Reed and everyone else in the room turned to the Premier.

Good. Reed knew that Whells agreeing with his explanation would make it easier to convince the Order.

"If we are to understand teleportation, we must first compare it to our current forms of transportation. Right, Doctor?" Whells gazed at Reed as though he were his college Professor.

"Yes," Reed answered, "Space-way for the last half millennia has been our main form of crossing between star systems. Hadn't this invention been made, it would still take roughly seven months to travel from Earth to Mars."

"So what?" a member asked, "Dowensky was able to create a faster way of travel than space-way?"

"Yes, but also no." Reed said, "Professor Dowensky, although troubled, he is still a brilliant mind. He created an unstable form of transportation, capable of moving an entire planet at a speed several times faster than light. To put it plainly, while Earth was hurtling from point after point within the universe, everyone on it would have remained at the same point in time. However—."

"For us, they vanished." Whells' words echoed in the room. Everyone looked at Reed with wide eyes. For a second it felt like one of the universe's secrets had spilled on the floor.

"It's hard to comprehend such a thing," one of the Order members spoke, "Frightening even."

The lady of the Order stood up, "I propose that none of this should ever be revealed to the public. If it were, fear would undoubtedly stretch across the universe."

"Doctor Doyle." The lady said, "The Order recognises your valiant effort throughout this investigation. Your contribution has helped us understand the dangers that have faced not only Earth but potentially the universe."

She looked at her fellow members, receiving a nod from each of them as she made eye contact.

"We, as members of the second sector of the Cosmos Order, hereby pardon you, Doctor Reed Doyle, for all past and *recent* wrongdoings. You are a free man now."

A month-long sigh left Reed's body, almost causing him to faint. He bowed before the members as formally as his body would allow. "Thank you, my Lords and Lady. I promise I'll continue my best efforts to work within the confines of the universal law."

"We hope so," the lady said, "for you may prove to be an asset in the next planetary matter."

"I would happily allow myself to be of use." Reed bowed again, mainly so no one would be able to see the fire in his eyes.

"There is a ship in the hangar bay," Whells said, "Take it and travel to wherever you please. Or if you desire, you may remain here and assist the Order further."

"My apologies Premier, but my place isn't here," Reed said, trying his best not to curse at the murderer.

"I understand." Whells bowed, "It's been an...interesting experience, Doctor. I wish I could see you off, but being who I am, I have a great many reports to write." He leaned closer so that only Reed could hear him, "and a promotion to prepare for."

Whells extended his hand to Reed as though he were a friend. He held a rare smile as he waited for the planetologist.

Flashes of blue plasma beamed across Reed's eyes, searing everything he'd seen in the last month. He saw the fighter ships descending upon Mars. He saw Whells' face twist as he smiled at Jessica's body. Everything the man had done was malevolent.

Reed shook as he relived each moment.

To kill Whells now would be a blessing to the universe. Reed looked down at Whells' hand, wanting nothing more than to slap it before shooting him in the chest.

It took Whells ten seconds to understand. "I see," Whells said with a smile. He turned to the members and bowed before leaving the room.

Good riddance.

"Is there something you wish to say, Doctor?" A member asked.

"Yes." Reed thought long and hard about how he was going to request such a thing, not knowing how they would react. They'd have their suspicions, but they had to remember that Reed was a man of science. It was natural for him to ask all types of questions.

Questions that he had for Professor Dowensky.

"I have a favour to ask."

***

They placed Dowensky within the same cell Reed occupied just a few days ago. However now, after some strong suggestions, the guard numbers tripled.

Doctor Reed Doyle stood within the room, watching Professor Dowensky lean against the cell's carbon fibre bars. The man looked defeated. He stared up at the roof with his eyes closed and arms hanging limp on the floor. He didn't speak when Reed entered, nor did he move in the direction of the entrance.

"Hello," Reed began, "I don't believe we've properly met. I'm—."

"Doctor Reed Doyle. I know." Dowensky bloodshot eyes locked onto Reed's. His gaze was sunken, his eyelids heavy with the weight of many sleepless nights. Reed recognised that look all too well. "I didn't think you'd ever allow yourself to work for the Order again."

"I wasn't given a choice."

Issac coughed a laugh, "There is always a choice. If it were me, I'd have flown myself to Eion," Issac spat on the floor, "Selfish bastards. Always doing the best for the universe. What a joke."

"You sound as if you've met them."

The Professor shook his head, "I tried to. Despite offering myself at their disposal, I was refused an audience."

"Why did you want to meet with them?" Reed asked.

"For the good of my people. Because I wanted them to hear my plan." Issac leaned back against the cell bars, "It was supposed to save them. I was supposed to save all of them."

For a while, Reed just watched as the years of loss consumed Issac, torturing and driving him to an unreachable goal.

"How did you do it?" Reed asked.

"When Theef was destroyed, I lost everything. Well, everything except a dimwitted sister and a fortune from my late parents. From there, I used our money to start a new life. We lived comfortably before I could begin funding my experiments."

"It must have been some fortune," Reed kept his eyes fixed on the prisoner, "after all, you were able to create time travel."

Stillness came from both ends of the cell room. Reed watched Issac's eyes shoot open and his head turn slowly like how a lion watches its prey. "How...?"

"Relocating entire civilisations. The time Earth disappeared for. Your reaction when we mentioned Earth was involved with the experiment. I thought I missed something, something so small that it could explain all the questions I had. And then it all made sense." Reed felt a bright light of pride strike his core, knowing that he was right in chasing his leads despite what everyone else said. "That demonstration you gave," Reed realised with a wondered smile, "you only presented it as a means of transportation for funding."

"Money is only good when you have a large quantity of it, Doctor," Dowensky said, "after that, one must find new ways to acquire."

"I truly believed you created teleportation," Reed felt stupid saying it out loud, despite how even more ridiculous the concept of time travel was, "Earth wasn't moving through space. It was moving through time, only to return a month later in the *exact* spot it disappeared from."

"It was only supposed to be me. I figured the best way to test it was for me to travel into the future. Less room for error that way."

"And instead, you took yourself and an entire planet."

"That was a complete accident. And one I never imagined," Dowensky looked away from Reed's eyes.

"You could have killed billions."

"I'm sorry," Issac said with a lump in his throat, "I apologise for bringing Earth into this. Had I known this would happen, I'd have held off on my experiments until I perfected the machine."

"Perfected?" Reed spoke as if insulted, "Time is only meant to move forward. To redirect its flow is to break the very laws of our nature."

"And what's so wrong about that?" Dowensky snapped, "Our universe is a flawed thing. Death, destruction, poverty, and slavery continue to inhabit it and grow like a virus. What is breaking the laws of nature if those laws are wrong? If I had succeeded," Dowensky continued, "my planet would be alive right now. Billions would be alive, as would their families, as would their homes. Why am I the one in chains, Doctor?"

Reed could feel his legs go numb.

"If you could go back and right your biggest wrong, would you?" Issac asked, "Would you save the planet you were responsible for destroying?"

A dagger struck at Reed's breast.

He'd never known someone who knew he was the one that caused Theef's destruction. Reed needed a second to calm his breathing.

The planetologist began to remember what the planet looked like the very second it exploded. He remembered what was going through his mind at the moment of detonation.

Screams can't be heard in space.

Reed was always fortunate that that was the case. To hear all the billions of lives die that day, Reed knew he'd have taken his own the second he had the chance.

"I do not hate you for the destruction of Theef, Doctor. As far as I'm concerned, Theef's time had come. Nothing could have saved it then." Issac stood up slowly and leaned against the cell bars. "But now it has a chance. We can change everything we know is wrong. By travelling backwards and forwards in time, we can save so many lives. So many planets."

The passion Reed witnessed in the Professor's demonstration lecture was reignited before his very eyes. It was true that with a working time machine, every global disaster could be prevented. Every wrong of humanity, everything Reed failed to prevent, could be reversed.

No. Reed shook his head.

"To break the laws of physics, as well as time, would mean risking the destruction of humanity."

"Not if we do it right," Issac said.

Despite how consequential Dowensky's enthusiasm was, Reed couldn't help but admire it. *I wish we'd met under different circumstances,* he thought with a saddened heart, *in another time, we'd have done so much good for the universe.*

"I've made a great many mistakes, Professor, some I wish I could go back and change. But we can't change the past. After Theef, I learned that actions have consequences, no matter what. And I will not allow myself to make another."

"Please," Professor Dowensky said, "you're not thinking right. Don't let them destroy all I have left!"

"I'm sorry." Reed said, "I really am. But it's over."

Rather than launch himself at Reed, the Professor began to weep, silently before growing louder and louder like a helpless child.

I'm sorry.

Epilogue

AFTER PACKING ALL HE brought with him, Reed returned to the laboratory. He found Roy, Pablo and Brandon all there, working on a new assignment.

"Doctor Doyle!" Roy jumped out of his chair.

The poor boy had a black eye and one of his arms in a sling. *What did the hell did Whells do to you?*

"Hello Roy," Reed said, expecting a handshake but receiving a hug instead. Pablo and Brandon came over with far less enthusiasm.

After a good but uncomfortable ten seconds, Roy let go of Reed. "You did it. I don't know how, but you did it," Roy said.

"Has Whells already talked to you?" Reed asked.

"Whells?" Pablo replied, "We haven't seen him since…"

Roy's face began to turn pale. What had once been joy stretched across his face was now replaced with grief.

"Did...did she suffer?" Brandon's voice was shaken.

"It was over in an instant," was all Reed could say.

Everyone took a moment to remember Jessica. It was easy to tell how much everyone missed the energy she brought to the lab.

"What are you doing here?" Pablo asked.

"I just wanted to say goodbye before I go."

"Go?" Roy asked, "Where?"

Reed didn't answer. Where was he going? His first thought was to return to Haple. After all, he'd considered it his home for the better part of two years. But for some reason, the idea of returning was no longer attractive.

"Hey guys," Pablo glanced at Roy and Brandon, "Could you give us a minute?"

"Huh," Roy replied cluelessly. Brandon however nodded and began to walk away with Roy's collar in his grip.

"Come on kid, let's make ourselves useful," Brandon said.

Pablo waited until the two were out of earshot. "So what's the plan?"

"What do you mean?" Reed asked.

"Come on, Doc. You can't expect me to believe you're going to fly home and pretend that none of this happened."

"I'm no longer needed," Reed said no louder than a whisper.

"Reed, if the last month has taught me anything, it's that the Universe will *always* need people like you."

Reed was ready to retort but stopped as he saw something floating outside the ship's window. It was Earth, shining with a perfect bluish hue.

You're back where you belong.

"Listen," Pablo said, "if you weren't here, we would have lost Earth forever, and Mars, for that matter. You can't pretend that we don't need you."

Pablo gestured at Roy and Brandon. The two had a brightness around them, a warmth that Reed hadn't seen before.

"I..." Reed sighed, "I don't know what to do. Or where to go"

"That's fine, we all make our way eventually. But just promise me you'll keep making days like today. The world is so much better with them."

"I promise."

Pablo patted Reed on the shoulder. "You've got a second chance, Reed. Don't waste it."

Reed gazed at Earth again. This tiny world was but a single planet inside an ever-expanding universe. To plan his next move was like catching a star "I won't."

***

Reed sat onboard a ship with no destination in mind. The only thing Reed could think of at the moment was Dowensky and how he only wanted to do what he thought was right. And because of that, he would be sent to Eion for millennia.

They got the wrong man, Reed thought, *I was the one who destroyed an entire world, and yet here I am, sitting on a ship with the free will to choose anywhere I want to go.*

Reed had a holographic map of every star system open in front of him. He didn't know whether it was best to return to Haple and go on from there or to choose a location at random and hope for the best.

For a second, he thought of going to Second Jupiter and opening a bar like Victoria, but that would only remind him of today.

Reed sat in the ship for some time, contemplating everything he'd seen and witnessed over the last month. He was a free man, a pardoned man, and yet he felt trapped more than ever. He looked at the map once more and saw not planets, but people, countless people who may need him, just as the people of Earth had needed him.

We move on from the past, and travel forward for a better future, Reed reached for the communication system. He clicked on all planetary channels. Reed took the coms with a shaking hand, unsure of what to say or how to say it.

He sat there, staring at the space in front of him and the planets that inhabited it. They needed him, maybe not now, nor in several years, but Reed knew he would be of use to the cosmos one day.

"This is Doctor Reed Doyle, astrophysicist and planetologist, contacting all inhabited planets. Some of you may know me. Some of you may not." Reed stopped for a second, feeling the grief of the past wash over him, "I've made mistakes," his voice cracked, "more than I ever thought possible. And because of them, I no longer thought I was worthy of protecting this Universe."

"But I know now that mistakes are what help us learn from the past. They are what help us make a brighter future. I might not be the man I once was, nor will I ever be. But the least I can do is try my best. So I call to you, whether you're from the farthest of galaxies or the smallest of worlds, if you are ever facing the danger of losing your planet, your home, your family, all you have to do is call me, and I'll be there."

Reed signed off from his message, clueless as to whether anyone was listening.

The planetologist put down the com system and laid back in his chair. He stared at the beautiful array of lights in space and admired the life that filled the cosmos.

Godspeed.